colour my grave purple

and other stories

SHEHNAB SAHIN

olive turtle

NIYOGI BOOKS

Published by
NIYOGI BOOKS
Block D, Building No. 77,
Okhla Industrial Area, Phase-I,
New Delhi-110 020, INDIA
Tel: 91-11-26816301, 26818960
Email: niyogibooks@gmail.com
Website: www.niyogibooksindia.com

Editor: Zinnia Sengupta
Design: Shashi Bhushan Prasad

ISBN: 978-81-990243-8-0
Publication: 2025

Printed at Niyogi Offset Pvt. Ltd., New Delhi, India

For you, Abba. Roohe Albi.

Contents

Author's Note

Colour My Grave Purple is a work of duality. A personal attempt to sift through sinking memories and pick unique storytelling ingredients from a fascinating part of India—its Northeast. It is also an attempt to codify the collective consciousness of the Assamese people and channelise it into a work of historical fiction. The former ignited the spark while the latter lent the firewood. The title may appear macabre to some as alluding to a symbol of death at the beginning of any work can seem unappealing. For many a well-wisher, this might even seem 'inauspicious', as this is my first work. Suffice to say that I want the title of my very first work to reflect a theme that has most significantly impacted my life, creating routes that would eventually lead me on my journey towards writing fiction—the death of my father.

My father, too, lived a life of duality. A police officer and an author. Two diametrically opposite professions squeezed into one mortal form that gave up quite early in life, both on me, at sixteen and on himself, at fifty-two. While alive, the late Khobir Ahmed represented many things for many people. An agent of authority, power and even fear in uniform and jubilation, hope, nostalgia and a plethora of other emotions with his pen. As he had published several short stories and seven novels in the Assamese language, it was a bolt of thunder for me when once, several years after his passing, I stumbled upon a dedication in one of his novels which read, 'For my daughter, Shehnab Sahin, who I believe does not like that I write.' Nothing could be further from the truth. Through *Colour My Grave Purple*, I wish for him to find this out. However possible, from wherever he is.

The ten short stories encapsulated in this work combine my love for history and desire to expand the narrative that travels from this part of India to the rest—that the core lived experience in the Northeast, particularly in Assam, is one of battling insurgency. The motive here is not to undermine the very real impact that insurgency has had on the sociopolitical and ethnocultural fabric of Assam. It is to very slightly diffuse the stronghold of insurgency as a dominant theme in the literary contributions from the region in general and Assam in particular. This fulcrum of insurgency and political unrest in Assam, especially in English-language fiction from the state, takes away from the various noteworthy experiences of the Assamese people that are worth sharing.

Another motivation to put together this collection has been to catapult 'frontier' voices to the centre stage of national history-telling. For long, both academic and non-academic writing about the Northeast, specifically Assam, has lingered on the peripheries of 'mainland' work. This was certainly my observation as a student of history, where for instance, chapters on the socioeconomic history of medieval Assam would be included in the *Appendix* section of a book. This lingering presence of Assam on the edges of the nation's historical experiences seems to have impacted fiction-writing from the state as well. Thus, themes that reflect regionalism and ensuing separatism and unrest are perhaps derived from this 'edge of existence'.

The history of Assam and its people is as meandering as the mighty Brahmaputra that flows through it. The stories in this collection are akin to the curves and bends of this ever-flowing river, signifying the resilience of the region as well as its people. A wide variety of themes have been used to craft these stories, such as the colonial plantation economy, external aggression, gender and social norms, human—animal conflict and insurgency, among others. Yet, they remain connected within the larger macrocosm of the geography as well as the universal human experiences of struggle and subsistence. *Colour My Grave Purple* makes an attempt to present a broad spectrum of these experiences that the Assamese have faced in their making of a modern, pluralistic society. The process therein has not only helped in building a syncretic society but has also aided in the preservation, expansion and flourishing of a unique Assamese identity.

The adaptability and strength of the people are dominant subjects throughout the collection. For instance, 'Two Leaves and a Bud' is set against the tumultuous backdrop of the 'top-down' introduction of the plantation economy in Assam. While mostly narrated from the perspective of a British colonial agent, the story lightly ropes in the persevering resistance of the plantation workers which obstructs the realisation of his duties. This tenacity of the Assamese people against both external and internal challenges recur throughout these stories which span a century. 'Ursula' is particularly interesting, for it places a real person and an equally real episode of external aggression in the centre of a fictitious narrative. Ms Ursula Graham Bower's journey as a single woman from England to the Northeast of India in the 1930s was no simple feat and what she did later was even more monumental. As an 'outsider', her intimate alliance with the Zemi Nagas of Assam reveals complex layers of Assam's history. Some stories focus inward as characters wrestle with their sense of self against the wider and oft merciless society, its norms and taboos, experienced through complex interactions with one's family and other social institutions. The story of young Pradeep, trying to navigate his queer identity in the 70's, upon the wave of a new cultural movement in Assam pivots on this theme. The ambitious timeline, from 1858 to 2019, assists in widening the scope of this collection to incorporate stories that surpass interpersonal relationships to the larger relationship between humans and the rich biodiversity of the region.

Having lived in several parts of Assam's countryside, I have personally witnessed the distinctive conflict between humans and the numerous animals that inhabit this bountiful place, the elephants in particular. I remember long queues of cars stranded in the middle of an elephant corridor, significantly delaying plans and schedules. I am often met with abject disbelief while recalling such stories from my childhood to friends and colleagues abroad. It remains a deep-seated desire to someday have all these skeptics stranded, not in the now-scanty elephant corridors of Assam, but the dreadful city traffic, where an elephant mounted by its *mahaot* would casually pass by!

Finally, *Colour My Grave Purple* is my ode to Assam. A song sung in remembrance of a place where once, almost every courtyard of an Assam-type house would be lit up by a thousand fireflies. A call to the foxes that used to howl right near the verandahs of police quarters and barracks. A smile at the rows of colourfully clad tea-pluckers, who had not a second to spare to smile back, lost as they may have been in their own song about their lands and ancestors in a faraway place. A deep inhale to retain the smell of the green tea leaves wafting through the air and the rusty smell of the red soil after the monsoon rains. While I embark on my own journey to understand what a home entails, this is my love letter to my first.

Two Leaves and a Bud (1858)

Gazing down at the steaming cup of orthodox tea cradled in his hands, Samuel Addington's mind kept floating back to the events of the previous night. Out with his bungalow servants to hunt down the mysterious leopard that had allegedly killed three of his plantation labourers, Samuel had almost reached the periphery of the Chinnamara tea estate, of which he was the manager. As they assumed their positions to keep watch, with an unusually sparkling full moon as the chaperone, an eerie sound wafted out from somewhere. Part music, part chant, it seemed to beckon Samuel to itself, like a sound from a concealed instrument awaiting its discovery.

Following the spectral sound cautiously, Samuel and his entourage found themselves amidst thickets of tea bushes much farther than the estate boundary where they had been preparing to shoot the erring beast. Up ahead, the labourers' colony could be spotted as a faint amber glow under an indigo night sky. When he felt closest to the source, Samuel gestured his crew to crouch and sneak a peek through the gaps in the bushes.

A small clearing lay in front of them, holding more than a dozen kneeling labourers chanting something unintelligible on repeat. The torches they held thinly irradiated a mud figurine fixed before them which was part serpent and part human. Standing almost four feet above the ground, a cloth turban was wrapped around the head of the figurine. Samuel was used to seeing such turbans on some of the Ahom noblemen on occasions.

Then out of nowhere, a man approached the figurine with a rooster in his hands. His face was unrecognisable and splattered with crimson. In a flicker, the man twitched the neck of the rooster, decapitating it, and poured its blood where the tail of the half human-half serpent figurine ended. The chanting got louder and just as the volume rose to fever pitch, the red-faced man drank the rest of the blood straight from the limp, headless rooster between his hands. With his heart pounding like a battering ram, Samuel gestured his crew to slowly and silently retreat from the bizarre scene. It was almost past midnight. As they briskly treaded back to familiarity, he heard his servants behind him gingerly telling each other, '*Dewan puja*...full moon.'

As he revisited the distressing memory from the night before, another part of Samuel's mind was a chequered chaos, tracing his journey in bits and pieces to this exact point in time where he was stuck in this unusual land, thousands of miles away from his charming Sussex. His mind patchily recalled the jolt of excitement experienced by the botanist in him on receiving his commissioning letter from the Royal Horticultural Society to study the *Camillia sinensis* in South-West China.

The China War that had concluded in favour of his country in 1842, three years before he began his own quest to the enigmatic Far-East, had opened doors for botanists to further tea research. Non-official British opinions were fragmented in assigning appropriate nomenclature for the war, some more comfortable calling it the Opium War. Samuel, however, thought it prudent to not ponder over causations. For him, whether the British and the Chinese had fought due to the latter's abhorrence of the opium trade mastered by his countrymen or because of the inimical treatment of British traders by the Chinese was inconsequential. What had mattered for the young Samuel Addington was his readiness to join the ranks of those that contributed towards empire-building. Even if that meant taking a serpentine journey across the Atlantic to research the tea crop and verify its ability to take root in locations other than hostile China. Samuel's thrilling job ensured that he experienced unfamiliar lands, languages, people, smells, flora, fauna, cuisines and diseases that spanned from China, Nepal, Bhutan and finally, to India, where he arrived with his prized Cantonese wife and a decade worth of experience in all things tea.

'The heat feels wet and heavy, Sammy, I cannot breathe,' his wife Mei Hui had proclaimed with bewilderment as they first landed in Assam.

This esoteric corner in the Bengal Presidency had been catapulted to the centre of the Empire's trading universe with the discovery of an indigenous variety of the tea crop. By 1855, the year he reached Assam, his countrymen had this wildly growing crop tried, tested, engineered, organised in nurseries and injected straight into the enterprise of satiating the swelling ranks of tea lovers in Britain. European planters alongside Company officials and native entrepreneurs began to eagerly explore this *tabula rasa* from which emerged the beguiling tea plantations as well as the joint stock venture, the Assam Company, to commercially produce the crop. This incipient enterprise, bursting with possibilities, gripped Samuel.

Driven by instinct to be bewitched by the foreign, the exotic, and the less understood, he found himself gulping the wet and heavy air that his wife condemned, which to him was dense with new promises.

'Your lungs will merrily adjust, my dumpling, just give it some time,' was Samuel's response to his wife's complaints.

On the persuasion of a company acquaintance, Samuel had joined the Assam Company as a crop surveyor, which was where he first heard about Maniram Dutta Baruah, or Maniram Dewan as he was popularly known. This was a name that inspired multiple, often confusing reactions among his colleagues. While some overtly spat out the choicest words befitting an ungrateful native, other quaint corners covertly murmured words of awe for a man who had been instrumental in introducing the Empire to this cash-pumping crop.

After the Burmese invasion of Assam in 1817, Maniram's family of noblemen had to seek asylum elsewhere and could only return with British protection when the East India Company forces began ousting the ruthless invaders during the first Anglo-Burmese War in the early 1820s. Upon returning to Assam, Maniram became a loyal associate of the British administration but continued to retain strong ties with the Ahom court, holding important titles like his ancestors and engendering a contentious reputation for oscillating between the services of the local Ahom Rajas and the Empire. Whispers remained afloat amongst colonial circles on how Maniram had introduced Robert Bruce, a Scotsman, to the world of the Singphos, a tribe that brewed and drank these wild leaves years before the arrival of either the plundering Burmese invaders or the British liberators. This contrived meeting not only irrevocably changed the local landscape but gave the Empire one of its most prized possessions, the *Camellia sinensis var. Assamica.* But just as fate is known to play unknowable tricks on people's lives, leading them to meander across uncharted territories, Maniram eventually found himself as a competitor to his patrons rather than a collaborator.

While posted as the chief land agent and executive for the Assam Company, he acquired crucial knowledge about commercial tea cultivation and eventually left his lucrative post to establish his own plantations, the Chinnamara and Selung estates in the upper Brahmaputra valley of Assam in the 1850s. For the company administrators, the likes of Maniram fit the caricature of someone who aspired for steady power by latching on to the dominant force in any given situation; the Ahom kingdom, the British Empire and finally, the Indian sepoy mutineers.

In 1857, Maniram Dewan conspired to reinstate Ahom rule in Assam by ousting the British with the help of the rebels. He was publicly hanged alongside a co-conspirator in February 1858, his beloved Chinnamara falling into the hands of the George Williamson Company a month later. But his legacy was nowhere close to being obliterated from Assam or his tea plantations.

Fate acted in similar, uncanny ways in Samuel's life as well. Within a few months of being a surveyor, he somehow found himself assisting the European manager of a newly established plantation, instead of only executing the tasks of his particular job. For a forager of novel experiences, this transition to a technical world of plantation, production, and transportation consumed Samuel fully, while distracting him from incidents like Mei Hui's three miscarriages in the last six years.

'Bara Sahab...Bara Sahab...' Gobindo, the head servant of the bungalow, softly called out, pulling Samuel back from this long mental journey.

'What is it?' asked Samuel, stepping away from the portico where he stood with his deep thoughts.

'The Hazira Mohuri Sahab is wait to see you the office.' Gobindo of the Kachari tribe was a nascent convert to Christianity and was rapidly improving his English, courtesy of his lessons with the missionaries and his zest for service. 'I tell you, Bara Sahab,' Gobindo whispered, 'We must bringing *ojha*[1] to bungalow. No ordinary worship last of night, *Sahab*. Yesterday Buddha Purnima and bad things can be happened, Sahab. The servants said me what they see and that you go bed when return. They too scare to tell, Sahab, but I wish your good. God knows what those labourers do. Some labourers have see too, *aadha* snake *aadha* man at night in the garden. Maybe it is not leopard, Sahab. We must get *ojha* to safe you and Memsahab.' Gobindo concluded his warning to his master in broken English, brimming with pride for having succeeded.

'Stop with your nonsense, Gobindo, and go fetch my reading glasses,' Samuel retorted, making his way to his study,

1 A colloquial term denoting an occult practioner in Assam

albeit forming a mental note to summon those servants later and grill them with a harsh interrogation.

The Hazira Mohuri was a supervisory office that kept the labour count and disbursed wages. But the register held by Nibir Phukon, the chief *mohuri* of Chinnamara tea estate, displayed mostly scarlet pages, with neat but closely piling scratches across rows of names. While waiting for the Bara Sahab, Nibir tried to memorise the names of the eleven labourers who were the latest in the long line of deserters from the estate. He wanted to appear diligent before his boss, not unintelligent like the other *mohuris* who referred to their registers for details that should dangle from their tongues. *Mohuris*, he thought, were in the elite services, after all, privileged to serve under European masters whose enterprising nature would turn Assam into a leading commercial center, perhaps like Manchester.

'*Mohuri*!' The curt sound of his designation snapped Nibir out of his trail of thoughts on Europe and its fairylike memsahabs, as white as milk. 'What is the early morning emergency?' probed Samuel.

'Bara Sahab, I apologise for this untimely call but I felt it necessary to inform you that eleven more labourers left the estate last night after an altercation with the *chowkidar*. They even beat him and broke his arm, Bara Sahab. He was taken to his home late last night. I visited him alone, Sahab, as you know, the other two *mohuris* are lenient towards service and probably deferred their visit until this morning. *Tch tch*. What misfortune seems to have fallen upon us, Sahab, with Chhota Sahab also taken with malaria. The *chowkidar* managed to get a few words out and told me how the deserters were accosted while leaving their colonies late at night without informing anyone. They had their families with them and on being confronted, screamed that they won't wait another month for their wages. This brings down the total labour count to 112, Sahab. Sahab, it will be extremely difficult to meet even one-fourth of our production target this month with the remaining labourers,' narrated Nibir, flushing as he failed to recall even one of the Kachari and Bengali names he had looked forward to calling out with secretarial finesse.

The recent outbreak of a crop disease which Samuel quickly identified as blister blight left nearly two-thirds of his plantation pestilential, affecting harvests and therefore labour wages. Despite efforts to mitigate the crisis with the fungicides Samuel laboriously produced with his own botanical expertise, the crops seemed unresponsive. It was almost as if the bushes wanted to carry those brown blisters on them and the young stems were cutting their life short on purpose, distorting and breaking off without the slightest contact. Wages had only been paid for four out of six months of the estate's operation since its purchase by George Williamson Company in March 1858.

While Nibir's monologue on problems of the plantation continued, Samuel was hit by a pang of despondency. When he had joined Chinnamara as the estate manager against the tumultuous backdrop of its owner's execution, a rushed auction and voluminous labour defection, his employers, the George Williamson Tea Company assured him of a quick return to normalcy. Samuel wondered at this point whether he had acted prudently or like a true imbecile in assuming his first role as an estate manager at Chinnamara, out of all the plantations that were frenetically brewing in the cauldron of Assam's upper Brahmaputra valley.

Under Maniram, Chinnamara had around 467 workers, mostly from the local Kachari tribe. There were also a dozen Chinese workers who were remnants of the first wave of skilled labourers that the company had brought from Malaya and Yunan. Apart from the Chinese and a handful of others, the majority of the workforce at Chinnamara had put their foot down in protest while the estate changed hands in an auction post Maniram's execution. Many of Chinnamara's workers had witnessed his public hanging alongside his compatriot Piyali Barua. Although mostly unable to make sense of big terms like 'treachery', 'conspiracy', or 'sepoy mutiny', most of the workers sensed that the new tombstone at Chinnamara under which their master had been hurriedly buried was an abomination; a potential harbinger of harmful consequences for all within its vicinity. The uncertainty that loomed over this particular plantation for its transfer from an indigenous 'rajah-like' figure to an unfamiliar company of *babus* prompted many of its workers to return to their paddy fields and their former plantation-free lives.

In the first week of the estate's transfer, 56 workers had gone missing. Within a month of the auction, when Samuel took charge, the estate was left with 220 workers for 270 acres of land. However, his benefactor's manoeuvres could ensure additional supplies of Bengali and Oriya coolies from nearby territories. Samuel was entrusted with this consolidation, which he felt confident about since promises of better terms for the old workers and regular wages for the new ones had brought the clock back to ticking mode, in sync with the timeframe peculiar to a plantation. But despite the dust settling after the torrential rain, a storm continued to brew somewhere on the sidelines, one imperceptible to the eyes, especially Samuel's.

'Announce to the labourers that they will receive the previous and current month's salary with a bonus equal to half of their monthly wage. They must continue to work without wages until the end of this month to be eligible for all of it,' Samuel declared, not knowing exactly how he would manage this, but sensing that this was the only way at that moment to check further labour seepage. As the *mohuri* skeptically took his leave to execute the orders, Samuel started a letter to the Superintendent of George Williamson Company, seeking immediate supplementation of the labour force and financial credit to cover at least another month's wages until the harvest of the remaining healthy bushes. How was it possible that the same plantation had produced 70,000 pounds of produce just a month before its auction, but just a few months after a change in ownership, its very existence looked perilous?!

Mei Hui had been watching her husband for a few minutes now. He was so engrossed with his vehement scribbling that he took no notice of Mei Hui standing by his office door, watching him intently. She waited until his pen was put to rest and whispered loudly,

'Sammy, I think we will make it this time.'

This startled Samuel, who turned around to see his expecting wife looking straight at him yet through him, sweat breaking out like tiny dewdrops on her smooth brows. It baffled Samuel how Mei Hui, who would resume her usual ardour soon after a tragic miscarriage, seemed peculiarly disoriented and fragile this time. For the first time, her pregnancy had entered its eighth month. Although cautious, the first few months were eased by the comforts afforded to a memsahab, with the uninterrupted attendance of the bungalow servants, soothing teas and foot rubs, sun-soaked portico readings of Byron and Keats despite her expressed disdain for the hot and humid Assamese weather.

In his attempts to prevent Chinnamara from falling into entropy over the last two months, Samuel had failed to take note of the thin cracks that had begun to appear in his otherwise composed Cantonese bride. It started with extended slumber, sometimes over twelve hours. Even when awake, she wasn't completely lucid. On several nights, Samuel woke up to an empty bedside and Mei Hui would be found sleeping on the portico with her eyes open. The next day, she would have no recollection of it.

What seemed like a natural forgetfulness borne out of her condition suddenly began turning a shade sinister. One afternoon, Samuel ran out of his study, following horrific bellows breaking out of the bedroom where Mei Hui was being attended to by a Kachari maid servant. He almost recoiled at the sight of the girl crouched on the floor, the burnt skin from her neck and shoulder distorting from the hot tea Mei Hui had poured over it. The mistress was annoyed by the maid's humming of a folk tune. An unthinkable act by a woman of faith, who had once led missions to spread the word of the one true and merciful God in her village in Canton.

There was once a linguistic departure to pure Cantonese for two days, where the servants' inability to respond invited a display of rage. Not even Samuel could request an explanation for the abrupt semantic amnesia as she would stare back, not comprehending, like a native would before an English-speaking sahab. On the third day, an exasperated Samuel found his wife reinstated to her usual linguistic abilities. When enquired, she responded with, 'Was I asleep for two days, Sammy?'

The previous night, after Samuel's return from the unexecuted hunt, he had found Mei Hui in his study, languid and humming the same folk tune that had cost that pitiful maid parts of her flesh. When her eyes met her husband's, she dashed out without as much as a hello, sobbing all the way to her room, incoherently mumbling something about not betraying the kingdom and saving the golden land from invaders. Watching his wife at this moment, however, standing by his study door, he knew she was his greatest achievement from his eastern sojourn, despite recent aberrations.

'What do you mean, darling?' Samuel asked her.

'I can feel him growing stronger each day. Oh, how he kicks, Sammy! This is, after all, the Year of the Horse. Our son shall be free and fierce in spirit.'

'How are you so sure it's a boy?' Samuel responded, looking curiously at his wife, who seemed the closest she had been to her true self in days.

'I just know, Sammy. I dreamt of his face 244 times in the last seven days.'

Later in the afternoon, post a routine round of the garden and the factory, Samuel summoned the servants from the night before, seeking a welcome distraction from his uneasy thoughts. By now, he was unmistakably worried about Mei Hui's rapid loss of lucidity. Somewhere, he harboured a sense of guilt for constantly dismissing her complaints about their present situation. While he was stationed at Bhutan for his research, a teaching opportunity in England had been extended to him. In Mei Hui's opinion, this was a thrilling proposition, more so for her unconcealed desire to experience England. Should he have listened to her more? Should he have cut short his oriental adventure and not forayed into this recondite valley? He tried to ignore the noise within him, borne from the battle between ambition and doubt, as the servants appeared, forming a horizontal line of three out of an unsaid order or innate habit. Their lowered gaze betrayed uncomfortable emotions rather than subservience.

'So, lads! What in God's name happened last night? Care to explain?' probed Samuel, as Gobindo, the head servant, eased their apprehensions with a broken translation.

'*Dewan Puja,* Sahab, *Bhado maah,*[2] season good, leaf bad, curse Sahab, leaf need blessing like medicine,' muttered one of them after a longish gap, very slowly, assisted by his compatriots in his hunt for the foreign words. Samuel's deathly glare pried open the next mouth which informed him, through a broken mix of three languages—Assamese, Bengali and English—that

2 The 6th month in the Assamese calendar which corresponds to the months of August–September in the Gregorian calendar

for some time now, various theories had been discussed by the garden labourers about the declining harvests and continually pestilential crops. The unanimously accepted theory, it seems, was put forth by the oldest labourer in the garden who had worked under Maniram since the garden's inception in 1845. He tried explaining, 'Sahab, tea leaf like *aatma* of true master. Master die, leaf die. Master and Chinnamara, same to same. *Ek aatma.*'

The bizarre explanations agitated Samuel. However, before he could unleash his infamous wrath upon the nervous labourers, Gobindo intervened, emboldened by kinship with the poor louts. Taking over from the others, he stated, 'Sahab, old labourers say, Master Dewan in rain and sun with tea leaf, Sahab. He touch leaf, talk to leaf, love leaf, leaf grow, Sahab. Leaf hear to Master Dewan love. Like father and child love.' He went on to explain how Maniram had apparently made a plea to the people of Assam to continue to look after his golden leaves after he was to be executed and the old labourers seemed convinced that the leaves had heard the plea.

According to them, the souls of the leaves had withered with their master's mortal remains. And so, it was only by keeping his essence alive that the worst could be averted for the garden and its keepers. Blood needed to be returned where from blood was taken. Hence, a minor animal sacrifice was required during full moons. One of the servants admitted to attending the initial ceremony but clarified that the main ritual performer had been different to the one they had seen last night, and he did not drink blood out of a decapitated rooster. They weren't sure who the people from the previous night could be.

It had been a few weeks from the day Samuel had heard the outlandish explanation from his servants. He knew of the peculiar beliefs that ran in this part of the country. He was also aware of the cult status of Maniram, but veneration with such tomfoolery was beyond his threshold of patience. There were real-world problems to deal with. Deserting and dying labourers, man-eating wild beasts, depleting accounts, unresponsive authorities, crop disease, excessive rainfall and a disintegrating Mei Hui were more than what Samuel could deal with at a time. There was hardly time to ponder over the cryptic beliefs and orchestrations of the ignorant natives. So the *puja* episode was shunned aside with no further deliberations.

Samuel was now at the edge of his endurance. The Superintendent had not responded to Samuel's last request and the latest harvest had produced the most deplorable leaves. Samuel felt as if a million strings were attached to his head and were all being pulled in different directions. Pacing in the ghostly silence of his study, he lost count of how much liquor he had downed to soothe his fatigued mind. He had entertained the thought of defecting to another garden some time ago, but the George Williamson Company seemed unnaturally interested in Chinnamara's success, and instead increased his remuneration. The economics of it all was greatly in favour of the company, given the abysmally low price it had paid for the garden's purchase. But to Samuel, Chinnamara was on its deathbed.

'Sahab, Sahab, Sahab!' A frantic thumping of his study door hit Samuel with how inebriated he really was. It was Minoti, one of the maids who attended to Mei Hui. 'Memsahab shout, Sahab,' blabbered Minoti, frantically rubbing her belly to communicate the circumstances to the listener.

Samuel bolted to the room where Mei Hui had gone into labour.

The sight before Samuel was more chaotic than he was prepared for. A profusely sweating and screaming Mei Hui, clutching the bedposts, was the synthesis of a melting wax figurine and a prowling cat. The moment he set foot into the room, Mei Hui's bloodshot eyes arrested his for half a second and in that moment, Samuel found what had been lost in recent history.

Half a second with those eyes, whose raven pupils were his seal of surety, of attestation, eyes that never lost sight of the empirical truth, that dreamt of Samuel's voyage into significance and of a life of true adventure. What endeared Samuel most to his wife was her ability to see things objectively. He felt sure that it was delirium that kept her from convincing Samuel of the futility of their present situation. He thought of this as he ran through the corridors to awaken Gobindo and the others to fetch the estate's doctor.

Stumbling over his own feet, he held on to the sills of the meshed windows to keep balance. He tried to quicken his pace, but a slithering sound suddenly arrested him to the spot. Despite his burning urge to keep moving, he found himself pressing his face to the window mesh, clutching its sills to still his vision, and looked hard at the lawn beyond, searching for the source of the strange sound. And then he froze. A turbaned head perched on a human torso was gliding through his lawn. The torso was faced away from him and as he focused his gaze on the rapidly disappearing figure, he saw its black, glistening serpentine trunk. The last thought on Samuel's mind was to never drink brandy on a hot summer night, as the bitter, frothing bile rushed into his mouth.

Gobindo's broad, porous nose was dangling close to Samuel's face when he opened his eyes. There was no way of telling how long he had been out of it. He squinted his eyes against the unending ambush of water that Gobindo kept sprinkling on his face. A hammer pounded his head. The second his consciousness rushed in, he lurched forward towards her room. A dozen bungalow servants trotted alongside him, like a pack of animals, silently but intently following a leader somewhere.

As he flung open the *sheesham* door, his eyes rested on a porcelain doll lying face up on the bed. Beneath the doll was a pool of blood that infused the room with a salty, rusty smell, amplified by the humidity. Two native women, one with a wailing infant and another with a cane fan, flanked both sides of the still porcelain doll. Silent as death itself, Samuel was rooted to the doorway, as the woman with a wrapped bundle walked towards him and handed over the crinkled being. With lowered, moist eyes, she spoke, 'Memsahab go, boy baby come.'

The crickets roared outside, and a gecko croaked, beckoning its mate to the room where Mei Hui's stiff, lifeless body lay. Samuel looked down at his son. He stirred ever so faintly in his father's arms, with a face that carried a tea leaf-shaped, port wine-hued mark from the outer corner of his left eye to the edge of his nostril. Crooning softly to the victory of survival, he moved in the same ether his father was now lost in.

Bellows of a Wilted Poppy (1860)

Rebo's state of mind at the moment could be likened to one of his concoctions; three spoons of powdered excitement, two pinches of optimism and a sprig of fear, diluted with distilled nervousness. While he waited for his patient, he rechecked whether anything was amiss from his repertoire: a scalpel, a piece of thin cotton gauge smeared in a paste of eleven herbs, a hair-like wiry brass string, disinfected cloth, hot water and finally, the analgesic—two goat pellet-sized balls of opium or *kanee*.

As a practitioner of medicine, Rebo firmly believed in the pursuit of peculiarities, of infirmities as well as cures. In his opinion, this was essential not only for progress in the profession but for the progress of man. Quite unlike his ancestors who kept their practice within the stale limits of simple colds, coughs, fevers, cuts, lashes and sometimes diarrhoea, Rebo pushed his knowledge of medicinal plants and potions much beyond his legacy. At twenty-five years of age, he was a highly accomplished *bez*[1] credited with curing ailments of the liver, kidneys, eyes as also non-organ disorders of speech and complicated curses such as infertility.

However, like his ancestors, he, too, believed that the spirits that could not find passage to the otherworld chose to inflict suffering on the bodies of those that remained on earth. There were common errors that humans made with such 'left-behind' spirits. For instance, urinating on trees inhabited by such spirits or leaving one's hair untied at noon in the middle of a paddy field. There were also some ailments that were caused upon fiddling with nature's laws, like eating cooked food during a solar eclipse, which most definitely eclipsed a woman's womb for life. Rebo felt privileged about having access to all kinds of *mantras,* which when combined with specific herbs and potions could take on the malefic effects of a spirit's wrath as well as that of nature herself.

Despite knowing these realities, he wasn't able to silence his curious mind, which kept asking him to look for causes beyond the habitual inflictions by evil spirits and remedies that could rely on things beyond esoteric chants. For a while now, he had been doing all kinds of experiments with *kanee.* In fact, the decision to deploy *kanee* in his practice served as a catalyst for many developments, especially in the treatment of extremely high fevers and extremely loose stomachs. Once he

1 A traditional medical practitioner in Assam

began administering studied doses to his patients, he realised that it was *kanee's* ineffable way of invading sensations of pain that helped push the boundaries of his practice. Sometimes, a bit too much. Like on this day, when he was about to enter an uncharted territory—the anus.

For a long time, he had come across complaints among his village folk, men and women alike (although he would never fancy any plans of treating women with such an unholy affliction!), of extremely painful, pus-filled boils near the anus. After a short period of being inert (although painful), the boil would erupt to discharge its contents in intervals. Soon after, the same contents would start oozing out of the anus as well. No cure was known for the condition and those cursed with the pain and foul discharge simply had to learn to live with it. Although rare, the few incidents of death linked to this disease impelled Rebo to pursue the infamous anomaly.

Rebo's subject for the day was the middle-aged village astrologer, Horideb. The painful abomination growing on his posterior made it extremely difficult for him to sit for hours and perform the laborious task of ascertaining the effect of celestial bodies on his clients' lives. He had tried several remedies, including treatment from the American missionary doctor of Sibsagar town. But the river of pus and blood continued flowing out of him unabated, like the river Disang. Until the very end though, he steadfastly avoided what soon appeared to be the only option left for him: Rebo, the eccentric *bez* from his village. He was aware of the *bez's* unorthodox experiments with opium in his treatments and because of that, he was extremely paranoid. But with his anal calamity spanning almost a year, something *had* to be done. The suspension of his business was finally beginning to pinch his pockets. Although more than the income loss, it was his wife's recent refusal to touch his manhood even over his dhoti, let alone perform her permuted fellatio, that finally pushed him towards Rebo.

❧

'*Probhuuuuuu-aaaaaa-oooooo...*' sang Horideb in pain and pleasure, as he lay on the bed, legs pulled apart by the two jute ropes that tied his ankles to the posts of the bed. It was another one of Rebo's creative ideas to prop his patient's legs up at a desired angle so as to maximise the exposure of the afflicted buttock area while minimising untoward interferences from the patient. Anyway, it was highly unlikely that Horideb could create any trouble for the *bez*. He was, at the time of the procedure, fully engaged with the apparition of a celestial fairy from Venus, who had begun stroking his hair and whispering titillating words into his ears moments after he had chewed a full opium ball. His patient's distraction helped Rebo in making a small but deep incision at the site of the discharge with the heated tip of the scalpel. At this, the bulbous mound instantly opened up, its contents flowing out with desperate velocity.

The sheer horror of what he was about to do next would have been unthinkable had his patient not reached his current state of *kanee*-induced delirium. Before proceeding, Rebo took a few seconds to stare directly at the face before him, which at that moment was breaking into spurts of giggles and soft moans, far from the hubristic expressions it was usually known to carry. Never one to want to be associated with the tag of a *kanee-khowa* or opium-eater, as those with the habit were called, Horideb's disdain for the substance was common knowledge throughout the village. After all, how could an irreducible Brahmin such as himself give in to sensory dictation by a substance easily accessible to and used by lowlifes? Horideb saw in *kanee* use a conspiracy by the low born to undermine the privilege of the high-born to enter spiritual realms, accorded solely to them by the Gods. Any claim of reaching such states was therefore a crime against the natural order of things, a moral corruption.

Unfortunately for Horideb, his choice pool of staunch moralists who abstained from *kanee* usage was quite shallow as poppy took root and blossomed in almost every social circle, from the boundaries of a paddy cultivator's home to the high walls of the Ahom kingdom's court. Rebo, however, knew better than to see the now bovine motions of Horideb's mouth with incredulity. After all, pain does different things to people. It demolishes, re-aligns, rebuilds dispositions. For better or for worse. He was unsure what the case was for Horideb.

While deliberating on this difficult disease, Rebo theorised several possible pathways to cures. For a while, most of his theories only stranded him in closed alleys as even in theory, the patient almost always died by pain-induced shock. If there were two ends for the discharge, Rebo deduced that they were connected somewhere by a passage, a drain which had to be closed. This would mean launching a probe, since no amount of theory could establish this conjecture. He thanked the heavens when the exact opportunity presented itself through Horideb's request.

Now prepared to put to test one of his most calculated theories, Rebo was excited as he took the hair-like slim, brass string he had disinfected and carefully inserted it in the opening of the boil which had just been cleared of massive amounts of pus and gore. The theory was that the depth of insertion would signify the length of the unwanted drain. By the looks of it, the site of discharge on his patient's buttock was quite close to his anal opening, a little less than two inches. As he began, his patient whimpered, shaking slightly, unable to do much with his bound legs. The absence of the anticipated howl prompted Rebo to probe further, although much to his relief, the probe ended very quickly. The drainage channel seemed no longer than two inches. If otherwise, he would have to think of other ways to close the passage.

Emboldened by this bout of luck, he confidently moved on to execute the last leg of his theory. He smeared the paste made of eleven herbs on the thin cotton gauze, wrapped it around the brass string and inserted it back into the passage with the calculated assumption that it would induce flesh growth in the area and eventually close the drain. Horideb shook and released a piercing wail this time. Nonetheless, the task had been accomplished without his patient passing out or worse, dying. Rebo concluded with a general *mantra* for healing as he was still uncertain as to what kind of spirit would cause such horror. He then waited for his patient to emerge from his state of stupor to tell him that the procedure needed to be repeated once every week to achieve the intended outcome.

'I think you are taking a very big risk here, possibly your worst so far,' said his younger brother Bonti later that night. Bonti was five years younger than him.

'And why is that?' replied Rebo, as he finished preparing his pipe.

'How can you perform such a tricky procedure relying only on *kanee*? I tell you, if it were me, I would have died just knowing what you were up to, let alone allowing you to do *that*. Besides, imagine having the blood of that village sweetheart Horideb on your hands. You could be lynched. I, obviously, would be dangling from the next branch!'

Bonti spoke with a tone betraying shock, distaste, paranoia and warning, all fused together in the rapid delivery of his statements. Lowering his voice to a whisper, he continued in a less severe and more mocking tone, 'How could you let your hands toil in *those* dirty fields of filth and plough with your fingers *that* row from which seeds are expelled and not grown. I mean, you eat with those hands and lick those very fingers!' He made a dramatic regurgitating gesture while pinching his nostrils together with his thumb and forefinger as he finished.

Ready to start recording the day's observations on a piece of birch bark spread before him, Rebo took a long, hard swig from his pipe and without looking up, spoke to his brother nonchalantly.

'He is not dead, is he? That's for your first concern. As for the rest of your worries, if my hands are soiled in that filth, what about yours getting rained on by the venom of your snake which you agitate almost every night? *That* is also an expulsion and I believe you eat with *that* very hand the very next morning.'

'What nonsense!' blurted Bonti. His cheeks were roasting in embarrassment as he shot back incoherent sentences at his straightforward brother while briskly heading for the door.

'Your stupid dreams...wild imagination...wild medicines...wild ways,' he uttered as he headed out, swearing to himself about replacing the bamboo partition between his and his brother's beds with a hard mud wall.

Rebo smiled, drawing in and blowing out another mouthful from his pipe, knowing that his big-hearted brother was incapable of holding a grudge against anyone, least of all him.

With his mind now effervescing on contact with the sweet *kanee*, intrusive thoughts began perching on those bubbles. This annoyed Rebo for this was exactly what was *not* supposed to happen. Involuntarily, he began pondering over the noticeable oddities in Bonti's behaviour of late. For more than a month now, Bonti had been spending most of his time in Sibsagar town which was almost two hours away from the village by foot each way. Not that he was kept unaware of the purpose behind this near daily travel. Apparently, his dear Bonti was guiding the foreign people in Sibsagar about the various uses of the medicinal plants that were found in his village.

Since their father's passing three years ago, Bonti had taken over the family trade of bartering their home-concocted plant-based medicines at the local market while Rebo continued to cure people's maladies with practices devotedly handed down to him by his grandfather. It was through one such buyer that Bonti had been led into the lair of the foreign people who called themselves missionaries. Like most people in the village, the only foreign people Rebo knew of were the sahabs. Their agents arrived punctually as per the season to collect a share of either his paddy or poppy as tax. His grandfather had told him stories about how the sahabs were invited to their land by their king to fight off the Moamaria rebels, pinning faith on the sahabs' large armies and fearsome weapons. But eventually, the Ahoms, whose ancestors were known to have descended to earth through a golden gate from heaven, were subjugated by these pale-faced sahabs by force of the articles they inscribed on pieces of paper.

Rebo had never understood how a transaction of this sort could transpire between two parties so unequal in descent. One with origins from heaven itself and the other from a boat where people fornicated in front of animals, as was told to him by his grandfather. As per his family's birch bark records, the last time they had a king was in the year 1826, which was nine years before he was born and fourteen years before his mother's heavenly departure during Bonti's birth.

Now sieving through tiny grains of memories—his mother's soft hair and warm touch—he felt a pang of pain for Bonti's lack of consideration towards their mother. He had missed nearly two weeks of the oblation ritual that was performed in their household for their dead ancestors every evening. This was very unlike his brother, who always made sure to wrap the betel leaf around the nut with a unique finesse before placing it on the offering plate. Rebo often joked that he was fighting to become their mother's favourite as she was known to have been extremely fond of her betel leaf and nut.

Rebo wasn't truly angry about Bonti's absence because he would continue with the rituals regardless, but to think that this was happening on account of his brother spending so much time with the missionaries was what worried him. These were some other kind of sahabs who had no history of helping the Ahom kings against the Moamarias or the barbaric Burmese. He knew from some of his patients that they were not of the same land even, and came from a place on the other end of the earth called America. That unlike the sahabs, they did not really concern themselves with becoming new rulers after the Ahom kingdom but wanted to do something even worse: turn the people against their own Gods and make them worship another God. One day, when Rebo asked Bonti if he was indulging in such mindlessness with the missionaries, he dismissed his brother saying, 'Why would I care about all that? They don't speak about such things to me and only seem interested to know about our plants and concoctions.'

Still, Rebo took this with a pinch of salt as the gossip around the village had not escaped him. A Batiram Das from a *kayastha*[2] family of his very own village now called himself Christian and carried an odd new last name: Peck. Trailing back to Bonti, he thought about the words he had pelted out, 'wild imagination, wild medicines, wild ways'. Why would he say that? Was he being told that their medicines, their ways were wild? What was un-wild? And what was wrong with the wild? Were the ways of the missionaries the opposite of wild? Did *their* ways have a deep reverence for their ancestors, an unshakable belief in the power of the cosmos, the known and the unknown that continued to influence the earthly planes, including minuscule spaces such as a household? Did the missionaries gaze upon the dotted skies and appreciate their own inconsequential acreage before the limitless celestial space that towered above? Could the missionaries even contact, let alone tame the creatures that lurked beyond the human plane?

From what Rebo understood, these outsiders still struggled to navigate through the vast bounty of Mother Nature, while the wildlings of so-called uncouth countries had been curing themselves of umpteen maladies through nature's agency for centuries. So why should the wild be senseless and the un-wild sensible?

2 A category within the Hindu caste system

Bonti, too, had questioned Rebo's procedure earlier in the day. In fact, this was the second time he had done this. The first time was when Bonti had asked Rebo to stop the practice of puncturing people's scalps with the sting of the *singi* fish into which warm, healing oil was poured to cure severe headaches (with a ball of *kanee* in the patient's mouth, of course). Many a time, Bonti himself had held the heads of the patients during the procedure. For him to suddenly question these procedures now was enough reason to suspect that all was not as innocent in the exchanges between Bonti and the missionaries as he projected it to be.

❧

'*Dhonyobad*,' said Jamini as he took the potion from the *bez*. Jamini's wife was down with the terrible yellow fever and as was known across the village, only Rebo possessed the quickest remedies. There were hardly any casualties at Rebo's hands, unlike with some others in his profession.

'That's fine,' replied Rebo stoically, which was his usual demeanor with patients and their wards. 'I had to pray over the potion from midnight to sunrise to strengthen its efficacy so make sure to administer it correctly. Apart from the potion, have her drink sugarcane juice once a day. Remember that the yellow colour of the fever is due to the *Halodhiya Khetor*, the yellow spirit that resides in her body currently. As you feed her the potion tonight, you may feel some disturbances caused by the spirit. Someone may keep knocking on your door at night. If it is three slow knocks, know that it is the *Halodhiya Khetor* trying to intimidate you. Do not answer the door at any cost. You may also suffer very bad dreams since you are the one caring for the host body that the *Khetor* inhabits. Do not pay heed. The black thread I tied around your wrist has protective spells which will minimise these things. She should be fine in a few days' time.'

Jamini let out a long sigh and continued staring at the mud-plastered floor of Rebo's hut. Rebo ignored him and started scribbling something on a piece of birch bark, hoping that Jamini would take note of his disinterest and leave him alone. After all, the *bez* was known throughout the village as a man of extremely few words, and the only conversations he engaged in were to do with symptoms and remedies for ailments.

Seeing that Jamini continued to stay put, Rebo reluctantly punctured the silence with, 'You should hurry on now. The longer you wait, the longer she suffers.' This roused Jamini from his thoughts, and he turned towards Rebo with a look of irritation in his eyes and said, 'All troubles come at the same time, it seems. Do you know,' he continued, 'that the sahabs are going to stop our poppy cultivation?'

Rebo was not sure if he had heard correctly. Inquisitively, he asked, 'What do you mean?'

'I mean that we will not be able to make our opium, let alone do business with it, the way I do,' replied Jamini, his voice acquiring drama. 'I take our home made *kanee* to the *haats* that are stationed a little beyond Sadiya, where the hill people from further east come down to exchange it with their forest goods. I know of a few merchants like myself who go as far as Yunnan with their own *kanee*. I only recently tied the knot so leaving my household for such long periods will not be appropriate.' The last line was spoken more to himself than to the *bez*.

Seeing a frown appear on Rebo's face, Jamini stopped his monologue momentarily, as if to relish the tiny victory of having captured the *bez's* attention.

He paused for a few seconds and resumed at a slower pace, 'What I mean to say is, stopping us from cultivating our poppy will be a disaster, especially for the likes of me and perhaps even you, seeing as *kanee* is an important part of your practice.'

'Where did you hear this from?' Rebo asked, his tone slightly curious but not animated.

'My uncle who supplies *kanee* to the *khansama*[3] that cooks at the Bara Sahab and Memsahab's bungalow at the Sonari tea plantation found out from the *khansama* himself. He told me about it later.'

---

3 A term with Persian origins, used during the colonial period to denote a cook, chef, steward or servant

'Pfff...as if a *khansama* will know about things like that. It is not just highly unlikely but nearly impossible that a *khansama* would be allowed out of a kitchen and at the table of the sahabs to discuss such affairs!' Rebo waved his hand dismissively in the air as he said these words, hoping that this bearer of such hollow rumours would take his leave soon.

Much to his dismay, the bearer continued, '*Arre*, trust me. My uncle told me that these servants at the tea bungalows learn quite a bit of the *sahabi* language, and it makes sense! They work so closely at the sahabs' service, after all. The *khansama* was told by a coolie who serves the sahabs their meals and teas, that his sahab and another sahab were discussing how they will stop us people from cultivating poppy.'

'Stop,' interjected Rebo, now a bit agitated. 'How is it possible that a coolie, of all beings, will understand what two sahabs are really talking about by just knowing a few stray words? I really have much to do now and don't have time for this! You, too, should rush to your wife.'

'Don't be so quick to dismiss this,' Jamini continued, ignoring Rebo's direct signal for him to leave. 'The Memsahab seems quite adamant about teaching her language to her servants as per the *khansama*, and it appears that our informant, the coolie, has gotten quite good at understanding it. He is supposed to have heard conversations on more occasions than that sahab-sahab meeting. Especially between a particular *Bogi*

Baideu and the Memsahab. This other white mistress comes down to the plantation from Sibsagar quite frequently, it seems, and reads the Bible to the bungalow servants in our language. They call her Mission *Baideu.* According to my uncle, the *khansama* sounded very confident while sharing this piece of news as he, too, is made to sit through these readings. And of late, it seems she speaks to them at length about "cleanliness". Not the kind you are thinking of right now, but apparently a cleanliness of the mind and soul, which tend to get filthy due to *kanee*. The Bara Sahab has also informed the workers that any *kanee* found on them will be exchanged with at least ten lashings of the *chabook*!'[4]

'Ufff…fine fine, I believe you, now please be on your way to your wife before the *Khetor* consumes her brain next. I really need to get on with work. What can we do if this is what the sahabs want?' Rebo drew Jaminis's monologue to a close with this. As the bamboo door of his hut flapped behind Jamini, Rebo went to the *Dam Khuta*, the central pillar in his hut which represented the resting abode of his ancestors' spirits. He squatted down on his knees before it and began chanting a long prayer to silence his mind, which was roaring at the moment.

The poppy that grew uninhibited in his family's fields had provided many an answer to many a question that Rebo

4 A whip

had had. In fact, he credited *kanee* for the success of several procedures in his practice as quite a few brilliant ideas were whispered into his ears by the healing fairy after he consumed it every night before bed. *Kanee* most definitely helped him leap from one risk to another, as in the case of Horideb, the astrologer who did, indeed, return the week after his first procedure to continue with the anal cure. Could anyone ever imagine attempting that feat, had it not been for *kanee's* effortless grip over pain?

Rebo was also extremely aware of another thing. Just like the universe hung on a beam of balance, he, too, had to find his own between being in his opium-induced spiritual realm and duty-bound temporal realm. For that reason, he kept his chewing or smoking limited to only two times a day. To think that this life he had known could possibly be upended by the sahabs was beyond him.

What right did they have to meddle with his people's way of life? They did as they were asked and paid their taxes to the sahabs. The sahabs, on the other hand, made themselves comfortable in a land which was far from their own, dominated their king, shaved off swathes of wilderness to grow tea, brought in strangers to look after that one crop, ordered people to work for them—all of this while not giving them anything at all in return! Only taking for themselves! In this scheme of things, shouldn't his people get paid their share of the profits made by the sahabs? Now wouldn't that be more sensible? As he wrestled with these thoughts, he made it a point to ask Bonti about the veracity of the story that Jamini had told him. His brother was happily and willingly entangling himself in the poisonous vines of the sahab's gardens after all. He might as well be of some use in getting further information.

Bonti had started for home after a long day at the weekly *haat* where he had managed to secure a very good barter. As he made his return by dusk, he was careful to avoid his neighbours' compound which was canopied by tall, thick tamarind trees. It was common knowledge that tamarind congregations must be avoided during evenings, especially at dusk, when malicious female spirits would wake from their slumber to look for unmarried males to possess. Once in possession, the man would have to forget all his chances of finding a wife, as the *jokhini* or evil female spirit would obstruct his every attempt to fix a match, through different antics. The worst one was lacing the victim's manhood with painful, pestilential boils so as to destroy any confidence he might have had in seeking a mate.

Indeed, Bonti had to be extra vigilant as he was intending to get rid of his bachelorhood soon. He was planning on telling

Rebo about his interest in Kanti *Khura's*[5] daughter Torali, so he could go as the guardian of the family and ask for her hand in marriage on behalf of his brother. Bonti was sure that he couldn't wait any longer for Rebo to get married and make way for him.

The whole village was gossiping about it. It appeared unlikely that Rebo would entertain the idea of marriage, despite his advanced age. His attachments seemed reserved for plants and potions and not females. It was not normal, but what was with his brother anyway? Bonti had been acting out in front of Rebo lately as his brother could hardly ever be caught at an opportune time to discuss the delicate matters of marriage, with his nose always buried deep in his birch bark or procedures. Bonti hadn't even found a moment to defend his recent delays in returning home, which were not on account of the missionaries but due to his dalliances with Torali. He was sure that his family in heaven understood and had agreed to the match already, for the relationship was moving on without any glitches. It was only with his brother that Bonti was apprehensive.

As he reached his hut, slowly building up confidence to broach the subject of his marriage before Rebo, he saw his brother sitting on the verandah, fanning himself with a cane disc made specially for that purpose. He looked sombre, which

5 *Khura* refers to one's father's younger brother, or a familiar elderly man in Assamese

wasn't unusual, but something about his demeanour was worrying. After setting aside the goods he was carrying, he sat beside Rebo and asked him what the matter was. Rebo wasted no time in narrating his conversation with Jamini from earlier in the day, as if he was just waiting for Bonti to return so he could unburden his thoughts.

'Is this whole thing true?' Rebo quizzed his brother.

'Hmmm, I am not sure,' Bonti replied, his mind already travelling to patchy bits and pieces of market rumours and conversations at the missionary press to see if there was something more solid there.

'What do you mean, "not sure"? That means there is a possibility that something like this might happen! Have you heard anything that could suggest this at that missionary press you go to?' Rebo pressed on, the concern in his voice clearly showing.

'See, I don't really spend so much time at the missionary press and most definitely don't understand what the sahabs discuss. But I can tell you this much; the interpreter who works there, Nidhiram Farwell, is known to speak against *kanee* to whoever he can catch hold of. He works alongside Mission *Baideu*, or Scott Mem as I call her, who is also the person learning about the medicinal plants from me. Nidhiram helps with translation mostly, although I must say the Mem is not that bad at speaking our language herself. Funny though, most of her sounds. *Phaat* for *paat*[6] and *meeh-lawn,* she says for *miholoni!'*[7] Bonti chuckled at the thought.

'Uff, stop digressing,' Rebo interjected. 'Tell me if you have heard something about the sahabs banning poppy cultivation.'

'Oh!' Bonti responded, as if jolted back to the present moment. 'See, I can only make inferences,' he continued, 'How will I know for sure about something like that? Although I do think there is some reason to suspect this may be true. Given that Nidhiram and Scott Mem are known to speak to the boys they teach at the Mission School about dissuading people they know from indulging in *kanee*. They supposedly visit people's homes, markets, even temples, to speak against the *kanee* habit. How do I know this, you ask? I came in contact with one such group at the weekly market last week. Some five–six boys only a little younger to me came up to where I was, busy bartering some of our herbs, and began asking me questions about the kind of herbs I had. I thought they were interested in buying, so I started describing them. When I got to our gooseberry and *kanee* mixture, one of the boys stopped me and said I should not be selling that. I asked why. He said that *kanee-khowa* is a filthy habit which is destroying our people. That it is ruining our minds, making us lazy and stopping us from realising the correct path.'

---

6 'Leaf' in Assamese

7 'Mixing' in Assamese

'What did you do?' Rebo asked, his tone serious.

'Obviously pelted stones at them until they ran like puppies. One of the pups made sure to turn around and shout that the sahabs will make sure to put an end to the "evil". So I guess we do have some reason to suspect that something might be coming up?'

Rebo listened intently to his brother. His bushy brows were now almost joined together in consternation, looking like one long caterpillar perched on his forehead. 'If this is the case, then it is something to worry about...' Rebo said as the sun made its final dip into a world unknown to both him and his brother, but he did not get up from where he sat. Bonti, too, remained beside his brother, although they usually stayed inside their hut during this time since it wasn't a very auspicious time of the day.

'Why would a Nidhiram Gogoi become a Nidhiram Farwell? Who even calls him that? How can people so easily abandon their faith? What kind of people come to the homes of others and turn them against their own beliefs?' Rebo poured out these sentences, sounding stricken with a sense of grief rather than with anger.

Bonti was silent for a while before he spoke. He had no answer as to why people chose to betray their own faith. He himself was not too occupied with questions of faith. He did what needed to be done, went about his life and that was it. As for the sahabs, he did not think much about why it was right or wrong for them to be around. Not that he remembered a time when they were not here. They were said to have arrived before either he or his brother were born. Since the only life he had known had always had the sahabs in it, how did it matter anyway? Unlike quite a few elders in his village who had seen a time before the sahabs, he, Bonti, had nothing to draw comparisons with. Not all the elders spoke highly of those times anyways. It appeared that the Ahom kings had fallen into decadence and could not protect the people from much. Now that their lives were not threatened, why dwell unnecessarily about such things, like Rebo did? He could not understand why Rebo held on so tightly to things of the past.

He feared admitting to his brother that even he was beginning to have some reservations regarding *kanee*. Unfortunate incidents involving *kanee* use were common throughout his village but they did not seem to have much of an effect on the people. Two months ago, his own friends Suseng and Kanak had gone missing after they smoked some *kanee* at an evening gathering with a few others. While Suseng's body was found by some fishermen three days later by the riverside, Kanak was never found. One of the boys present in that gathering later described how Suseng and Kanak had had a long, euphoric discussion on the traits of true warriors and had decided to test theirs by swimming across the river at night.

What had begun to truly disturb Bonti was how so many men, young, middling and old, were spending most of their days doing nothing but making merry with *kanee*. Their fields were untended, their animals neglected and families overburdened with additional work. He himself loved the occasional escapes he made with *kanee* but it looked like not everyone had his kind of resolve. Now that Bonti was planning on starting a family too, it was all the more reason to stay away as much as possible.

'Maybe it won't be that bad if we were not allowed to grow poppy. Perhaps it is time that we compose ourselves and go back to working in the fields the way our ancestors did, expertly flattening uneven lands for our rice fields, not an inch out of place,' Bonti commented, looking straight at the distant fields from his veranda, where fireflies glittered like stars in the night sky.

Rebo did not answer for a while and continued looking in the same direction as his brother. When he spoke, his tone was calm, despite dripping with bile. 'I was right then, Bonti. You, too, seem to have fallen into the trap laid down by the sahabs. One by one they take away what's ours: our land, our people, our faith, our way of life. It is not for them to decide whether we should take *kanee* or not. It is not for them to tell us to follow another faith, dip our heads in our very own rivers and then change our names to theirs. Is this why you have missed so many days of our evening oblations, because you are too busy forgetting that our ancestors need to hear and see us pray for them? Are you so busy getting to know their God?'

'What are you taking about?' Bonti now turned to face his brother and looked straight into his angry eyes. 'I told you, I am just teaching them about our medicines while they give me a few goods in return for the favour, like the mustard oil you burn every day in the earthen lamps for our ancestors. You don't seem to care about anything other than your potions and patients so it is I who needs to keep things running in the house.' Bonti wanted to say more but decided against it, as they were not used to talking to one another this way. Never had they had any open discord or confrontation as neither interfered with the other's trades or practices. With no precedent of such incidents and without any clarity on what to expect from Rebo, Bonti decided to withdraw.

Just as he was about to get up from his sitting posture, Rebo spoke, 'I make sure to keep our family together by honouring our forefathers through my practice of medicine and faith. I never questioned your lack of interest until now. But you have not only questioned my practice of late but have also shown utter disrespect to our ancestors by missing so many rituals.' Rebo spoke quickly this time, sweat breaking out on his temple as he, too, was uncomfortable with confrontation.

Seeing an agitated Rebo, Bonti softened. He could not imagine a time when his brother had looked this distraught and hated that he was responsible for it. He decided that it was the moment for the truth to set him free. He said, '*Xuna*,[8] I have been late for the oblation rituals for all these days because of an entirely different reason. I have been taking a longer route to our house around the *Dangor Pukhuri*, the big pond.' He paused here for a bit, unsure of how to go on.

'Why?'

'That's where Torali...Kanti *Khura's* younger daughter goes to fetch water before dusk,' Bonti replied slowly.

'And why would you do that?' Rebo pressed on quizzically, still not comprehending his brother's hints.

At this, Bonti looked towards Rebo once again, this time directly meeting his eyes. With a frustrated look, he went on, 'She fetches water from there every day at a particular time before dusk because she *knows* that I will be crossing from there. That's when we meet. This has gone on for a month now. It took a whole week for her to notice and another to finally smile at me. I'd be late for my own funeral for that smile,' he concluded, looking at the back of his hands resting on his knees.

This made Rebo smile. It was as if a huge boulder had been removed from his heart. It was not the allure of the sahabs that

8 *Xuna* means 'listen' in Assamese

kept his brother from home, but a woman! *That could be easily dealt with*, he thought, and turned towards his brother to say, '*Hobo*,[9] I will ask an astrologer to look at the charts first thing in the morning tomorrow to see which will be the most blessed day and time for me to speak to her father to ensure we get a yes from him.' Bonti tried to suppress his smile as he nodded and made for the door of their hut.

The blessed day arrived forty days later. Bonti's marriage was fixed with Torali without any mishaps, as was destined to happen based on Horideb's reading of Bonti's birth chart. What Horideb had also predicted that day was some kind of doom to befall their people soon, so an early date for the marriage was deemed essential.

Today, as he sat in front of a fresh piece of birch bark, Rebo's mind looped around the events of the recent past distractedly, which most definitely seemed like a prelude to difficult times. A month ago, the sahabs did ban private cultivation of poppy, only allowing the sale of *abkari* or excise opium. Those wanting to sell had to purchase some kind of license from the authorities. People were only allowed to buy from these licensed sellers.

9 *Hobo* means 'okay' in Assamese

Bonti was proven wrong. He had been increasingly doubting the benefits of *kanee* in people's lives. He foolishly thought that banning *kanee* was perhaps decided by the sahabs to make the *kania*[10] work more, be productive. Well, if that was the case, then why would they want to sell *abkari* opium?

What was essentially free before, now had to be purchased. People went in swathes to purchase *abkari kanee*. In just a month, Rebo began noticing how some of his neighbours, who would earlier use their homemade *kanee* just like him, suddenly seemed casually preoccupied with how, when, where and how much of it could they purchase from the shops. Some like Rebo remained undeterred and continued growing their own poppy openly in abject defiance while some pursued it in secrecy.

Some of his village acquaintances seemed satisfied with these changes, such as Jamini. His pestering, gossiping client had acquired a sellers' license from the authorities. Jamini was due to meet Rebo for a consultation that day. Rebo thought it wise to finish recording his observations on the *bakul* bark's healing quality for bleeding gums before Jamini arrived and put a stop to his writing flow with unending news and petty gossip.

'O Rebo da! I come bearing great news!' exclaimed Jamini as he entered Rebo's hut, holding a packet wrapped in a banana leaf.

10 A negative term in Assamese used to denote an opium user

'Is it?' Rebo responded with utter disinterest.

'Yes, yes! My wife is finally expecting and I want you to make the most divine potion to ensure that a strong son grows in her. Also, please accept these *pithas*[11] and laddoos she sent for you,' he thrust the leaf-wrapped packet into Rebo's hands before taking a seat on the floor.

As was quite customary with Jamini, he quickly jumped onto an entirely different topic and asked Rebo why he was still growing poppy inside his compound. If noticed by the authorities, he would most definitely get in trouble. Rebo said that he couldn't care less and if he was ever questioned, he would tell them straight that it was to be used for his medicines and that it could not be helped. He said that he was not the only one acting in defiance. Many like him continued to grow it in their own compounds and make their own *kanee*.

Jamini felt it necessary to clarify, that despite his earlier reservations about the sahabs' intentions, he was quite content with the present order of things. The license that he had managed to secure made life easy for him. He beamed while adding that only 'respectable' members of society were allowed to bid for the license. He no longer had to travel far out to the frontier beyond Sadiya to trade with the hill people. He could stay home and sell it—now that people couldn't cultivate their own (barring those like Rebo who were clearly taking a

11 A rice-based dessert made on special occasions

huge risk), they thronged to such shops like bugs. Business was booming, he said.

But did Rebo want to hear some other interesting news? How the sahabs were hardly getting a breather from back-to-back attacks on their property? The Singpho tribes had attacked two tea estates the previous month. No sahabs were injured or killed but vast tracts of the plantations were set on fire. The worst incident, albeit a little funny, took place at the Sonari estate. Once again, he had heard this from his uncle who was a supplier for the garden.

'Last week there was a small get-together in the Bara Sahab's bungalow. Not many people. Just Mission Mem, her husband, their friend, and Bara Sahab and his wife. The coolie who was serving them was the same as the one I told you about earlier. The one who has become quite good at understanding their language and commands. It seems he was called in the middle of some discussion by the sahabs and informed that a new name was chosen for him. After the river-dipping ritual, which was scheduled for him in the next couple of days, he would no longer be known as Bhula Tanti but as Joseph Levi.'

Jamini paused a little, as was his style of narrating gossip, hoping to dramatise it for the listener's benefit. Seeing no reaction from Rebo, he then continued, 'Something about that must have hit the coolie's otherwise empty brain,' which was what the *khansama* had told his uncle.

'As the rounds of tea turned to wine for the Bara Sahab, Scott Sahab and the friend, Tanti mixed a copious amount of *kanee* in the blood-red liquid. For the memsahabs, he laced their milk tea with it. In less than an hour, the masters dozed off where they stood or sat! When they awoke around dawn, the sahabs reeked of urine, which was showered upon them generously by our brave coolie. Memsahab supposedly fainted right after she woke up, courtesy of the previous night's memory and the foul smell on her bonnet. She has been sent to the Khasi hills to her sister's place to recover from shock apparently. A dozen coolies along with their families, probably led by their supreme commander Tanti, deserted Sonari that night.'

Jamini interlocked his fingers, twisted them back until they snapped in harmony and concluded his story with, 'Such nonsense...' Rebo grinned from ear to ear as he opened the leaf packet and popped a sweet coconut laddoo whole into his mouth.

Freedom in My Blood (1920)

No one had ever told Mamoni that blood would come out of her body's 'dirty part' someday. Her mother had often told her in no uncertain terms that the body part where the blood was now coming out from was *dirty*.

She had been playing a hopscotch game with her friend Pranati across boxes she had drawn on the ground with a twig. It was Pranati who first saw the blood. She was standing behind Mamoni, who was hopping ahead to the last row, when she noticed a red streak quickly dripping down Mamoni's left leg. She let out a loud gasp that made Mamoni falter mid-jump. Annoyed, Mamoni was about to charge her playmate with cheating but before she could, Pranati blurted out, 'Your leg is bleeding.'

As Mamoni looked down at the uneven red line making its way towards her ankle, she began looking for the source. As she pulled her frock up to discover the source, she was shocked by the findings. A blankness engulfed her mind for a few seconds before she gathered up her frock in a bunch over her *dirty part* and began a sprint back home, leaving Pranati to wonder if her friend's sudden predicament was the outcome of her chanting. She had recently learnt from her grandmother, a famous *ojha*, that chanting a certain phrase nine times while imagining the colour red weakens the strength of the enemy. She had been determined to make Mamoni lose at hopscotch that day, although a sense of guilt had begun to creep into her quickly, like the bottle gourd growing in her grandmother's garden. With this, she made her way back home, reminding herself never to chant like that again, even if she were losing. Making someone bleed seemed like a step too far and the sight of blood made her feel queasy, even if it wasn't on her own body.

When Mamoni appeared before her mother who was sifting rice flour on the verandah at the time, she could only manage to make some unintelligible sounds, unsure of what to say. As her mother's gaze travelled from her face to the bunched frock and finally, the dried rust-coloured streak on the leg, she gasped and said, 'So soon!', more to herself than to Mamoni, casting aside the sieve almost aggressively.

She took Mamoni to the well and asked her to wash the blood off of her body as fast as she could, all the while throwing furtive glances around her. She would have done it for her, but touching her daughter in this condition was forbidden by tradition; it was considered *chua* or impure. Besides, she could not afford to break any more rules at this early stage. As it is, she was allowing her daughter to touch water, which was not allowed for the first three days. But she was more progressive than her peers. It was late in the afternoon and most people were inside their houses anyway. Hopefully, no one would see them. She then led her daughter to the smallest room of their tiny house where Mamoni's father, a head teacher, kept his books and a few other things utterly unsuited to their mud house with a thatched roof.

Once in the room, Mamoni's mother started doing things in some sort of a practised sequence. First, she closed all the curtains in the room. Next, she spread out a cloth sheet on the floor and sprinkled some water in all four corners of the room. Finally, she turned towards Mamoni and made a revelation, 'You are a woman now, Mamoni. But first, take a look outside the window and make sure to rest your eyes only on a mango or coconut tree.'

Mamoni peered out of the window through the small opening her mother had made by parting the curtain very carefully, so as to not let her daughter's incipient womanhood escape from the room to the wide, bright and frightening world outside. Mamoni's heart was pounding, for she could somehow spot neither a mango nor a coconut tree despite crossing those very trees every morning on her way in and out of the house. She felt her eyes lose focus with the fear of this sudden incapacity which felt like a crime, and started blinking frantically, as if rapid blinking could conjure up the desired tree. Her mother shaking her arms and asking, '*Hol ne, hol ne*, are you done?' was not helping, so she blurted out, 'I can just see a betel nut tree, Ma.' To her relief, her mother said it was okay.

'You see, when a girl becomes a woman, she must first look at a fruit-bearing tree. The bigger the fruit, the better is the capacity of her womb.' Mamoni's mother felt reassured that her daughter had at least managed to look at a symbol of fecundity, unlike one of her nieces, who was in the paddy field when she turned into a woman, with no fruit-bearing trees within sight. Hence the affliction of only one stillborn in her seven years of marriage. It was true that Mamoni was only ten and such an early transformation was unexpected. But where does one stand against the will of providence?

Mamoni was unable to comprehend anything her mother was saying and was too frightened to ask about what was happening to her. Was she sick? Was she wounded during her hopscotch game? How? She hadn't injured herself anywhere. How long would blood be coming out of her *dirty part*? Were her parents supposed to take her to Doctor *Khura*, her father's friend who cured everyone of everything? Her mother had put some folded cloth between her legs. What was she to do with it? What did her mother mean by 'when a girl becomes a woman'?

Weren't all girls women? Despite the barrage of questions in her mind, she only managed to ask her mother, 'What am I supposed to do now, Ma?'

Her mother informed her that she was to stay locked in this room for the next three days, eat only raw food, which would be served to her in the room, sleep on the ground on the sheet laid out for her, and under no circumstances whatsoever was she to look at either her elder brothers or her father, not even through the window of the room. Mamoni took all of this in with a serpent growing inside her chest. What was happening? How was she to remain inside a locked room all by herself when she had never even slept alone in all her ten years? The serpent began to glide around her lungs, making its way to her throat, which stung as she processed her mother's words. The loud questions swimming in her head were making her slightly queasy and the nibbling pain in her lower abdomen was not helping either. All she could think about as her mother bolted the door from the outside was whether she would be able to see Gandhiji, who was to visit Guwahati five days later. She had memorised the date. August 10th, 1921.

That night, almost everything inside Mamoni hurt. Her stomach, not because of the nibbling pain from earlier, but from the unfulfilling meal of fruits; her neck, arms and back, from the hard mud floor beneath her; her face, from the impact of the cold creeping in through the thin cloth sheet; and her chest, from the snake which had grown quite large by nightfall. Her mother had not come to her room until quite late in the evening and that too only to pass on some fruits to her through the window. But as she spotted Lord Krishna's idol on the table inside the room, she rushed in to grab it. *Hari, Hari,* she chanted, clicking her tongue as if regretting a grave mistake. Before bolting the door shut again, she made sure to interrogate Mamoni about whether she had touched God after her *chua*. Much to her mother's relief, this act had not been committed, and Mamoni was informed that 'turning into a woman' meant that she was impure for some time, so touching God while she was in this state of impurity would be an unforgivable sin. She was also told that she would be 'dirty' every month for three to five days for several years and that she was to memorise all the things her mother had said to her that day before she went to bed.

Mamoni writhed on the floor all night, her eyes wide open and ears alert to any sounds coming from outside the window facing their garden. More than her mother's words, she was repeating a chant she had learnt from Pranati which could cast away evil spirits and ghosts.

Goosebumps were appearing and disappearing from her skin like twinkling stars, as thoughts of the demon that murdered children kept popping up in her head. Conflict tore at her whilst she chanted, for she was also a big girl who was aware of names like Mahatma Gandhi, Jawaharlal Nehru and Gopinath Bordoloi. How, then, could she succumb to lowly fears of ghosts and demons?

She was disappointed in herself. It was all a façade, she thought, her *bigness,* and it crumbled like dried cowdung cakes in the dark isolation that surrounded her. Her thoughts kept going back to the common knowledge in her friend circle that when children lied too much, especially to their elders, the child-murdering demon kept count from atop the tamarind trees, where he resided during daylight. There were many tamarind trees where Mamoni's family lived. Come nightfall, the demon would descend, locate the homes of the lying children, push his serpentine hand in through their windows and suffocate the criminal while they were asleep. The hand was known to lengthen until it found its prey. There were no known deaths among her friends yet but as per most of their parents, several such murders had taken place during their time and they passed on the message quite diligently to their own progeny.

As a matter of fact, Mamoni was burying a deep secret within her heart. She was in the habit of throwing away the milk that her mother gave her to drink on most mornings. Sometimes, she was compelled to gulp down that tasteless, white abomination but most often, when her mother wasn't looking, she would sprint out of the kitchen to their backyard and fling it into their pond, knowing any evidence would drown.

That night, she cursed herself. She wished she could take back the lies she had been telling her mother about finishing her milk, and how smartly she would dip her finger in the liquid and dab her upper lip with it to make her lie convincing before flinging everything into the pond. Her mother would tell her brothers and her that many people would willingly give their father precious things like milk without expecting anything in return. He was a very respectable person after all, as the head teacher of a local school for boys, and people looked up to him. It was only her husband's idealism and aversion to the idea of debt that kept him from accepting such gifts from people. He consciously used his very meagre income to buy milk for his family. Mamoni may have been called and treated like the 'little one' in the family but she felt 'big' enough to understand that sometimes, her father could not bring home a lot of food.

Her vigil against the long-armed demon began thinning around the crack of dawn. A heavy exhaustion blanketed her, pinning her to the floor, disallowing her tossing and turning, her eyelids betraying her will and descending like dark, laden monsoon clouds. As she began slipping into the sweet suspension of sleep, her last thoughts were of her father.

Her father, a tall, gangly head teacher, eager and stern while teaching even his own children. Her father, who occasionally took the thin bamboo stick to the calves of his sons when they failed to produce the outcome of a simple multiplication sum, but never on Mamoni, no matter how many times she failed him. Her father, who often talked about sending the white people back to their own homeland, which, as she was told, was as far from Guwahati as the moon was from their home. Her father, who brought a spinning wheel, diligently spun cloth and made his wife do it too, expecting an estimation of the amount done at the end of each day. Her father, who spoke incessantly about Gandhiji and wrote about him in pamphlets which he distributed among their neighbours himself. Her father, who had promised her that he would take her to see Gandhiji, who was as respectable as the head priest that their family went to, only he was the head priest of the whole country.

Mamoni awoke with a very uncomfortable wet feeling between her legs the next morning. It was a bit like a few years ago, when she would wet the bed at night. Yet something was different now; it was thicker. She was aghast to see that blood had seeped out of the cloth between her legs to her frock and the sheet beneath her. A big, red, unfamiliar stain stared back at her. She was annoyed and angry, and tears welled up in her eyes. Hunger ate at her stomach and her body ached from the most hostile sleep of her life. She got up, stood by the window of her room and called out to her mother, at first pleadingly. By the time her mother arrived, she was shouting and sobbing.

Her mother, instead of comforting her, gave her some fresh clothes along with a few commands. She was to use a fresh pile of cloth between her legs and change the sheet on the floor. A door in that room opened up to their backyard, which she was to use to wash the stain off the sheet with a cauldron of water her mother had provided. She was to keep her eyes lowered while doing this, as under no circumstances were they to chance upon any passing male in the distance. She was not to wash herself, except her hands and mouth, in order to eat the fruits which would be served to her.

To Mamoni, these words were harsher and more painful than the ear-wringing she was used to getting from her mother on being caught doing something naughty. She had never washed clothes before in her life. She had never had to sleep on a cold, hard floor and had certainly never been bolted shut inside a room. This uncalled-for appearance of blood from her *dirty* body part was the worst thing that had ever happened to her. It seemed like becoming a woman meant having your life turn extremely unpleasant. Maybe that's the reason women cried so much.

A few months ago, one of her friends, Setona, had turned into a woman. That was all Mamoni was told and no one at the time had explained what exactly had transpired to 'turn' Setona into a woman. Her family was invited to attend a wedding ceremony for Setona which had frightened the daylights out of Mamoni. Setona was her friend and a little girl just like her. At the ceremony, Mamoni could not locate any arrangements made for the arrival of a groom. Instead, it was only Setona, dressed in traditional bridal attire, perched on a low stool between two banana trees, holding a brass plate with betel nuts and leaves for the guests. There was a feast and the environment was congratulatory. Mamoni was thoroughly confused, and when she coaxed her mother with questions, she was simply informed that this was Setona's *tuloni biya*, or upliftment wedding, where her ascendance from girlhood to womanhood was being celebrated. There was no groom involved in this and soon, the same thing would happen to Mamoni as well. When Mamoni pressed for more information on this one-of-a-kind wedding, a particularly bad ear-wringing put a stop to any further questions she may have had.

Later that evening, Mamoni heard her parents get into a bad argument; bad, because never before had she heard *both* her parents engage in equal tempo with one another. Eavesdropping from behind the window of her room, she heard her mother say, 'You know that she turned late in the afternoon, and that she is between *Ugro* and *Hostini Kanya*[1] as per the priest, which means she will have an extremely challenging married life. Do you want to make it worse than it already is? The *tuloni biya* can only take place on the seventh day and under no circumstances can she leave the house before that. Taking her out of the house on the fifth day would be a disaster for her, a total disaster!'

'The time and date of a woman attaining puberty does not determine how her married life turns out, her temperament and upbringing does. As she has inherited her mother's temperament, there is no escaping a troubled marital destiny for her anyway,' her father retaliated, his words dripping with a harsh, cold spite.

'How can you be this cruel? You don't care about your family, that is very obvious. What matters to you most are your meetings with people that just talk, talk, talk...your writings and Gandhi. Have the foreigners gone? As far as I know, they are still squatting here and we are still carrying the shit out of their chamber pots. You have stopped going to the school and only go around in useless processions, taking our sons along and forcing me to spin endless rounds on the wheel and for what? Do you think Gandhi even knows your name? And now

---

1 According to traditional Assamese Hindu beliefs, the time of day when a girl attains puberty goes on to determine the nature of her marital life.

you want to take Mamoni into one of these, knowing that you will be jeopardising her whole future?' Mamoni's mother was heaving as she delivered the last of her taunts.

'Do not cross your limits! I don't intend to be a father that treats his daughter as a creature of foul and obsolete traditions. You want to keep yourself chained to them, that's your decision, but don't impose them on our children. As for Gandhiji, my name is of no consequence to him or the credo of Gandhism. Nor those of our children. A saint does not know the name of every follower he has. It is the aura, the uncontaminated energy of his being, that illuminates the lives of all his disciples, who are tuned into him without name or face or any visceral connection. Just as I am, just as our sons will be, just as I want Mamoni to be. I promised to take Mamoni to Gandhiji's procession and that is what I will do.'

'Over my dead body.'

This retaliation from Mamoni's mother brought a stalemate into their war of words, but the last was still to come. After a few minutes, Mamoni's father responded in a softer, more sombre tone, 'I have never been known to be an unreasonable man. I have conceded to your wish of locking her up, even to having the *tuloni biya*. I understand that on the fourth day, you will be giving her the ritual bath. Have all of this. On the fifth day, she needs to be out.'

He left the room with these words, as Mamoni's mother let out sobs as disturbing as the sound of howling foxes on a moonless night.

Mamoni spent the third day of her isolation with several happy thoughts. Part of the joy sprang from the knowledge that a ritual bath customary on the fourth day of turning into a woman meant a release from her prison. It did not matter to her that she would still not be allowed to touch or be touched by anybody until the seventh day; if the thought of her exit from the room had a taste, it would taste like honey. The other part of her good mood was from being told that she would be allowed to make her own boiled rice and lentils and eat it after sunset. What a relief! Never in her life could she have imagined salivating so vigorously at the thought of boiled lentils. She was grateful that she knew how to cook the basics, or rather, grateful to her mother for scolding her relentlessly until she had learnt to make these things. Finally, the knowledge that all was not lost on the Gandhiji front made her heart leap with unadulterated joy.

Mamoni was enchanted by her father and all the things he did. She especially loved to hear the stories he told her at night before she fell asleep in his arms. About the poor

Tejimola, who was killed and buried by her evil stepmother when her beloved father was away. She later re-emerged from the ground she was buried in, in the form of a bottle gourd plant, and justice finally found Tejimola in inexplicable ways. The stories of the terrible Burmese invading Assam a century ago fluttered before her often-sleepy eyes, a scene full of noise, grime and destruction, inspiring a gratitude for the peace that she enjoyed in the present, at home in Guwahati.

She was particularly intrigued by the stories her father told her about the white invaders, the British, especially since these were far from fables. That these white devils lived amongst them, stole from their country and were somehow living like kings despite the thievery, enraged her. She had seen them on one occasion, when her father had agreed to take her to town to show her a printing press. A few men—as white as the milk she threw away so frequently—were on horses, marching in file. When a tattered-looking mendicant came close, one of the marchers drew out a bulgy baton and struck him. Anger flared in Mamoni's veins as she could relate the scene with several stories that her father had told her of how these invaders set fire to villages that refused to pay them with a share of their crops, how they beat and flogged people in the tea gardens and how they called her people *dogs*. They had to go back to where they came from, she thought.

Her father often told her that they needed the support of Gandhiji to do exactly that. He called Gandhiji a *Mahapurush*, a great man with the qualities of a saint, who could make hundreds, no, *thousands*, of people believe in one cause. Her father told her brothers and her that Gandhiji was the only one who had the power to throw the British out of their country and that they should all do as he commanded. And what was the command?

The command, as her father would say, was to stand righteous against the enemy. How to stand righteous against the enemy? To this, her father would respond with an illustration. 'Imagine an angry, brutish man is beating a poor, helpless farmer. You witness the beating and realise the unfairness of inflicting pain and suffering upon the weak. You decide to intervene and stand between the brute and the victim. Now you are receiving the blows instead. It hurts you but you do not flinch. You get hit again and again, making you weak in the body. You get a very bad blow straight to your knees and you fall, but you stand up again. When the brute realises that no matter how many times he hits you, you will still rise, he begins to feel tired. He gets tired, because every time he hits you, it strains his arms as well. If he must keep at it, eventually the blow will begin to lose its force, making him look weak to his enemy. What does he do then? Perhaps spit out a few curses, but then, he exits the scene. That, my dear child, is when you attain victory.'

'If you keep getting hit, your bones will break, your teeth will shatter, you may bleed. How can you keep getting hit and keep rising?'

'That strength is what Gandhiji is teaching us and for that strength to come to you, my child, you must always be truthful.'

On the fourth day, Mamoni was dressed in a simple *mekhela* and made to sit between two banana trees. The ritual that was to be performed signified Mamoni's further ascendance into womanhood and for that, it was important to have witnesses. Her mother invited a few women from the neighbourhood as was customary, and the occasion took the form of a small celebration. The women sang a few lines from wedding songs that lamented the loss of a daughter and her journey to the unfamiliar home of strangers. Different varieties of lentils and raw turmeric pastes were prepared for the ritual and smeared on the exposed parts of Mamoni's body. Although it was quite early in the morning and the humid August air made breathing an effort, the touch of the cold water from the well sent shocks across Mamoni's skin. She flinched with each splash but felt relieved at the end of it all for the serene sense of cleanliness that wrapped itself around her. After she dressed herself in a fresh set of clothes, she wasn't remotely expecting to hear her mother command her to return to her room.

'Why? Yesterday you said that from the fourth day onwards I can leave the room and stay within the house.' Mamoni felt the serpent in her chest awaken as she spoke.

'Stop asking questions. Do as I say,' Mamoni's mother spat back, her eyes wide and black with spite.

Mamoni hated her mother in times like these. Her mother, who usually pinched her daughter's cheeks teasingly, cuddled her at night and generally spoke with a sweet disposition to everyone around her, could turn into a whole new person when questioned. Be it her husband or children, on being questioned, her usual sing-song tone would suddenly acquire a scathing brassiness, transforming her into someone entirely different from what she had been only moments earlier. Mamoni was wary of this side of her mother. Her resolve to demand her freedom from her mother effervesced away at this point and she could only manage to whimper, hot tears prickling her eyes, 'But, but...'

'You are a big girl now, Mamoni, stop crying like a little one.' Her mother continued. 'I am doing this for your own good. You did not turn at the most auspicious time and this will create problems for your future if you do not atone for it properly right now. Our priest had prescribed a seven-day isolation for your *chua* but you will do only four days as your father will take you out tomorrow.' Mamoni's mother sounded tired as she said that last sentence, but continued. 'As a woman, you will have to make many sacrifices and this short isolation is only the beginning. Trust me, this is the only way your future as a wife and mother stands secured.' She ended on a softened note, perhaps suddenly touched by her own sorrow of witnessing her child grow.

Mamoni did not care for her mother's apparent sorrow and howled as she reluctantly went back to her prison.

Despite the defiant howls aimed at her mother and her continued detention for becoming a woman, Mamoni felt much more at ease on the fourth day, because the next day would be the fifth and last. It also helped that her stomach had stopped being assaulted by raw fruits and sprouts but was newly warmed by something cooked, no matter how frugal. She paced the small room, her father's so-called study, every now and then. She counted the hours. It was nightfall and only a few hours remained for the next day, for the procession. She felt reassured and jubilant with the knowledge that her father would take her to the procession the next day, no matter what.

She wondered whether Gandhiji liked Assam. Did he also wonder, just like Mamoni, about how deep the Brahmaputra was? Surely he would see the river! To reach Assam, he must have come riding on its currents. There must have been hordes of people at Sukreswar Ghat to catch a glimpse of the great man. Or would Gandhiji find the water too ugly? She knew from her readings that there were seas and oceans in the world with water as blue as the sky. How pretty that must be! Her father had told her that Gandhiji had lived in foreign places far, far away from India, even in the land of the white devils. He must have seen and touched ocean water and revelled in its beauty.

The thought made her sad, but where was the time to dwell on sadness? She had to start preparing for the procession. Would all the people in the procession be marching? 'Left right, left right…' she stomped her feet and marched to and fro in her little prison. Then, she lit the oil lamp on her father's desk, took out a paper and slowly scribbled on it, 'Dear Gandhiji… Jai Hind…' and stopped. She did not know how to proceed further, since there were a lot of things she wanted to convey, which meant a lot of writing, which meant a lot of effort. She did not like writing long things. She wanted Gandhiji to know how very excited she was to see such a great man and how she would join him like her father and brothers and drive the British out of her country. That she was aware, as her father told her, how the British people got scared when thousands of Indians gathered in one place and made them feel like outsiders, and that she would be willing to join those crowds. Mostly, she wanted Gandhiji to know that her father loved him the most, more than all their neighbours did, and that she hoped to see her father stand next to Gandhiji with her own eyes. She wished Gandhiji knew that she knew about the great people of Assam who had died fighting against the enemy; even women, like Kanaklata Barua. Did Gandhiji know that?

As the night sky darkened and an owl hooted outside, draped in the thickness of a *nahor* tree, Mamoni fell into a deep slumber, with a barely scribbled parchment clutched firmly in her fist.

The fifth day heralded a significant era for Mamoni—a time from her childhood, that would bear its imprint on several moments of her future. At first, the fifth day delivered to her the undulating sensation of hope. Of feeling elated about possibilities that could come true with every passing second, of a door unbolting at any minute; as hope has a way of uplifting and letting one down all at once.

The fifth day delivered to her the weight and power of time. How time is the sole edifice on which all else in our conscious life rests; how experiences like hope, anticipation and exasperation are simply playthings for the mysterious phenomenon of time.

How when time decides, hope transitions into anticipation and then exasperation, and when this happens, all one can do is cling onto time itself, like a child to its mother.

The fifth day delivered to her, lessons on love. How quickly it ebbed and flowed, in and out, when all you had known of love before was its steadfastness and permanence. The fifth day delivered to her the complex choice that is faith. To have faith in a thought, a dream, an idea, a person and how faith demanded more from you than love itself. How to love in faith when the door, despite the promises made, remained shut throughout the day.

Ursula (1943)

Ramgakpa the soothsayer was rather unimpressed by the size of the python that was being carried into the *morung*[1] by ten boys. By the looks of it, he estimated it was about fifteen, sixteen feet long and about half the width of his outstretched arm. The night before, he had already had a vision about its size in his dreams. As a result, there was nothing new about the sight in front of him.

Besides, he was nearing his retirement. He would have retired a decade ago, had it not been for the exasperating devotion of his fellow tribesmen. Of late he had begun to consider his glorified ancestry somewhat of a curse. Six generations of soothsayers before him had led the inhabitants of Laisong village into gullies of good health and wise decisions through near-accurate predictions and spiritual healing. While those before him (as he was told) had relished the gift of the 'third-eye' with zealous fervour even after crossing over

1 A tribal term for a youth dormitory

the revered centenarian line, he was already exhausted at the youthful age of nine and seventy. He had plans for the life he had left ahead of him: to explore and study the mystical worlds of the different varieties of mushrooms that dotted the forest. He was sure that no one from among the eighty households at Laisong had stumbled upon the colony of odd, owl-like mushrooms spreading like weed behind the bamboo groves. On consuming one out of curiosity, he had been transported back to his past life, when he was a raven or a kite, looking down on blue-green mountains and river valleys, not dissimilar to home. It took a few hours before he snapped back into his current incarnation and decided to dedicate the rest of his life to understanding the magical world of mushrooms and impart the acquired knowledge to his people. This would be his legacy.

The python was released in the big, dusty courtyard of the *morung*. The young residents of the dormitory along with elders invited from the village made a circle around the serpent as it slithered and skid about, its bulk slowing it down. The poor creature had no way of knowing that very soon, its head and tail would be severed by the sharpest *dao*[2] and its skin would be hung on the walls of the *morung*. No room for much sympathy though. For it was the creature's destiny to meet this end while aiding the village

2 A single-edged sword used commonly in Assam

in foreseeing its future through the patterns it created on the gathered dust.

Ramgakpa was studiously observing the patterns. Keeping his eyes fixated on the python, he started to scribble symbolic notes with a hard twig on the dusty ground before him. But first, the customary details: the human year 1939 and beside it, the shape of his tribe's totem, the bull, depicted by two sharp projectiles emerging from each side of an inverted triangle. He had to admit, the patterns were quite confusing this time. Bow shapes, *dao* shapes, spear shapes all combined together into the intended message.

What could it be? He tried to carefully disentangle the dusty mess before his eyes and attribute meaning to the individual patterns. When he finished, he gasped, and said three words: *queen, war, memory.*

Reliuyile couldn't stop thinking about the woman. While out foraging in the forest with her family, while bathing in the crystalline cold stream on the fringes of the village, while plucking the feathers from the dead body of a duck, and especially while she went back to the *morung* to spend the night with her dormitory peers.

Reliuyile had become a member of the *morung* six months ago, when the number of fingers she had stopped indicating her age. Like every other girl in her village who came of age, it was now customary for her to join one of the youth dormitories. There were similar dormitories for boys but she had never been inside one. How could she? It was the boys who were allowed to visit the girls' dormitories and not the other way around. She didn't exactly know why and certainly couldn't ask her mother.

Custom expected them to spend the days with their own families but come night, it was straight to the *morung*. Several girls slept in one big room. Some were similar in age and some older. There was a headgirl at the *morung*. She was largely nice and particularly patient during the singing and dancing lessons. She did not yell or beat the younger girls as was known to happen in some other *morungs* of nearby villages. But her affability flipped completely if someone so much as sneezed during bedtime. She expected the whole *morung* to fall asleep at the same time. The sleeping orders would be executed like a drill, with a firm call for everyone to return to their cots from wherever they were. Most girls would be out in the courtyard, chatting about everything under the sun—from the boy from the nearby *morung* who had expressed an interest in so-and-so girl to the perfect threading of a loom pattern by another.

After the call, the headgirl made sure to turn off all the lamps herself. Once darkness descended, nothing but deathly silence was expected. Only the snorers were exempt. If two or more girls were caught whispering or giggling, they were made to sit outside the *morung* all night. To make sure that the punishment was adhered to, the head girl punished herself as well, by keeping watch over the punished girls. Reliuyile often wondered how this was a valid punishment, for the punisher was never the one meant to suffer. She had learnt this from her mother, who had often barred her from attending village feasts or made her peel a hundred onions at a go as punishment. On those occasions, only Reliuyile suffered, her mother certainly did not. On the contrary, the headgirl suffered every time she punished someone. This confused Reliuyile. She had so much to learn.

A week before, the strangest thing to ever happen to Laisong had happened, causing Reliuyile to lose all her focus. A very strange-looking woman had come to sleep at the *morung*. Her skin was the colour of the rice powder Reliuyile helped her mother grind, with hair the colour of jute crowning her head like a man's! She was tall, and wore the strangest costume, with cloth that wrapped both her legs individually. The first night she slept in the *morung*, no one snored. Reliuyile knew this because sleep came to her only when the roosters crowed the morning to light. Perhaps sleep evaded many that night, for it was most unusual to have someone so strange amidst them. She was dropped at the *morung* during dusk by Namkia.

Everyone in the village knew Namkia. He was the only one from the village who had left home to work for the sahabs in Haflong. Reliuyile had only heard about Namkia in passing but that day, she saw him in person for the very first time. There was nothing strikingly different about him, as Reliuyile had assumed would be the case. He looked like any other person from the tribe. Stoutly built; skin the colour of rust; smooth, thick, straight black hair that fell over his ears. Namkia did, however, manage to shock the daylights out of Reliuyile, when she heard him speak to the strange-looking woman in a bizarre tongue. How a Zeme Naga learnt to speak something like that was beyond every ounce of her comprehension.

When curiosity got the better of not just Reliuyile, but several other girls from the *morung*, they hounded the headgirl before bed time, as she had been seen welcoming the strange woman into the *morung* earlier in the day along with a few other elders from the village. The mystified girls were informed that this was a Memsahab who came from a land very far away. They were told that seas had to be crossed on vast ships to go where this Memsahab came from. These girls knew neither sea nor ship and could only visualise their village stream as a boundless body of water that started from the village but allowed no one to see the end.

The morning after the Memsahab's arrival, the headgirl rounded up the girls in the room and gave them clear instructions that they were expected to process throughout the day before their return to the *morung* at night. They were to steer clear of the Memsahab and not disturb her at any cost. They could communicate with her only if they were approached by the Memsahab, although the headgirl rushed through this instruction lest her timorous tone be noticed by the girls. Perhaps the headgirl was worried about this part more for herself than the other girls since her stature at the *morung* meant that she was the one most likely to get asked things by the Memsahab. This would be nerve-wracking for anybody, not merely for the lack of language but largely due to the sheer reality of being in such close proximity with someone who seemed to be from another realm. The renowned poltergeist of Laisong village—known to wail a terrible tune on moonless nights, scaring away cattle and humans alike—seemed a more familiar figure than this Memsahab.

It seemed that the Memsahab was at Laisong to study their people and would be living in the village for a while. She would be living in the *morung* until a special camp for her was built. This piece of news caused one too many murmurs to float about the tight spaces between the huddled girls, annoying the headgirl a little. *What does it mean to study people?* someone asked. That someone was told to shut her stupid loud mouth and do what she was told.

That week, while the Memsahab spent her nights and sometimes days at the *morung*, Reliuyile burnt with many curiosities. She couldn't stop thinking about the articles she saw on the Memsahab, like that metal box she would sling around her shoulder, at times pull close to her eyes and make a *click* sound with. No stretch of Reliuyile's imagination could help her inquisitive mind decipher what it was that the Memsahab saw when she peered into that metal box. If only she could somehow find the object alone for a minute...

The opportunity presented itself before Reliuyile when one day, the Memsahab decided to accompany a few girls from the *morung* to the secluded stream for a bath. All the way to the stream, Reliuyile had sidled along, keeping her eyes quite fixated on the metal box that was swaying with the Memsahab's hips, hanging on a contraption. Once there, the girls ushered the Memsahab to a clearing with large rocks whose dents, fissures, formations and arrangements had been used by the village women for safekeeping for centuries. The metal box was kept amidst such rocks, at a safe distance from the water.

Reliuyile waited patiently, like the leopards that lurked on the fringes of their village, only to pounce on their cattle at the most opportune time, leaving no evidence of the victim. Reliuyile was clear that unlike those conniving leopards, she was doing no wrong; merely giving into her weakness of touching things she was not supposed to. Once the Memsahab reached a fair distance from where her belongings were, Reliuyile leapt out and flung herself between the rocks, hiding her frail form like a chameleon in the cracks of the massive stones. There it was. The metal box. She went closer and without a second thought, reached out to touch it.

Nothing. Very normal.

Like touching a pot while boiling water back home or feeling the hard surface of the rice pounder beneath her feet. What had she expected to happen after she touched it?

She lifted the object with both hands, then held it out in front of her. Like the Memsahab usually did, she then brought her face close to it and squinted her eyes.

Nothing.

She then took her index finger and ran it in slow circles around the smooth round surface. She quite liked the sensation. Engrossed in the action, she didn't know whether it had been only a few seconds or several minutes before she felt a tap on her shoulders. She leapt away, like a feline caught sniffing fish, and found herself face to face with none other than the Memsahab herself. She was laughing and muttering some unintelligible words to Reliuyile.

Her mind was racing and her face throbbed hotly. For some reason, she decided against running for life and stood fixed to the spot, staring back at the Memsahab. The next thing she knew, the Memsahab had come closer to her with the sack she had used to carry her belongings to the river. She sat down on the smooth surface of one of the rocks and took something out of that sack. She then turned towards Reliuyile and motioned for her to sit down next to her. Reliuyile felt her feet move despite herself as she slowly walked towards the Memsahab and sat down next to her.

She dared not look at the Memsahab's face but was intensely aware of who she was sitting next to. Her body smelled so different. A sly peek at the Memsahab's arms revealed a haphazard array of brown spots, as if a handful of cumin power had been flung at her and it had settled on her skin. The fine hairs on her arms shone golden under the sun. As Reliuyile was revelling in these new anatomical discoveries, the Memsahab put her arm ever so gently on Reliuyile's shoulders and showed her something unlike anything she had ever seen before.

Right in front her eyes were Namkia and a dog, only they were a hundred times smaller in size and appeared flat and stiff on a paper. Reliuyile gasped! The Memsahab let out a soft laugh and shook her head. She then replaced the flat and stiff Namkia and the dog with another such paper where Reliuyile was aghast to find the exact replica of her *morung*! *Just what kind of sorcery was this*, Reliuyile wondered. Many more flat pieces of paper were then placed one after the other before her, some with faces of people quite like the Memsahab's, pale and otherworldly. As she absorbed all of this in absolute silence, the Memsahab started speaking again. The words made no sense to Reliuyile.

'These are photographs, my darling girl. Would you like me to teach you how to take them?'

On seeing no response on the face of her subject, the Memsahab then tried another tactic. She turned her full body towards Reliuyile, looked her directly in the eye, placed a hand on her own chest and said, 'Ur-su-la.' She repeated this three times, progressively slower each time. Reliuyile finally felt some sensation returning to her dry throat and mouth and almost involuntarily, felt the form of a sound leaving her mouth, 'UU-SU-LA.'

The bull was one of the biggest the village had ever seen. The ferocity in its eyes augmented the aura of its strength. It required nearly six men to hold him just about steady and tie him up for the night. The traditional bull chase for the season was to begin early next morning. Daogankpa's *morung* had lost the chase for the last three years consecutively. This year, he had taken it upon himself to disrupt this unholy trend and lead his *morung*, his comrades, on the golden path of victory. He had been working hard for it too.

For the last three months, he had silently worked on his strength, waking up at the crack of dawn, running for miles and miles, up and down the undulating hillocks and focusing on his axing duties as a means to strengthen his arms. After all, it was the arms that carried the central responsibility of holding, restraining, pulling and harnessing the voluminous beasts.

Apart from this self-imposed training, there was also a growing confidence among his *morung* regarding his natural strength, which had been missing for the past few years. He had bloomed unusually late. Just a year ago his appearance had been rather frail, his lanky height not supported by any muscle volume. To manage this transformation, he had done something that he vowed to take to his grave and hide from divine providence itself. He had sought counsel from the old witch, the village outcast living on the edge of their settlement, and agreed to swallow two raw bull testicles whole as she chanted her incantations. He had paid her with two black fowls which he stole from a neighbour. The risk paid off, and his magical mutation started to make itself visible day by day. It was true that many of his friends teased him incessantly; some even pulled nasty jokes, attributing his rapidly changing appearance to his manhood finding release with monkeys instead of girls, as his face was considered ugly by many. He never lost his cool and took solace in knowing that deep down, these boys were jealous of how tall and strong he was now. In fact, for the present year, he was adjudged as one of the lead contenders for the bull chase with some of his *morung* elders betting on him to bring in the much-awaited trophy.

It was during one of these morning runs that the 20-year-old's eyes fell on the most exquisite sight. A fairy walking by the woods with a hairy dog by her side. He was shocked and spellbound simultaneously. He slowed his pace and started walking, nay, *padding* like the snarly cat in his family home. It dawned on him pretty quickly that what he was looking at was the famous subject of ongoing village gossip. The arrival of a Memsahab among them. He was the only one who had not seen her yet, having had no opportunity to.

Her hair was glistening golden ever so lightly under the soft morning sun. She was taller than almost all the village women *and* men and walked funny. A little like a duck. She did not look old at all, but also not as young as his 16-year-old sister. Her clothing was strange, too, but covered most of her except her arms. Every now and then, she stopped to look at the trees around her or pick up things from the ground and put them inside a bag that hung sideways from her shoulder. She was also carrying a strange-looking thing— a square metal box which she would bring close to her eyes at times while standing stationary. He wasn't half as curious about the objects on her as he was about her.

Smitten by how fair the skin on her arm was, he did not quite realise when his steps sped up and he wasn't as far away from her as he would have liked. At one point, she turned around suddenly. On coming face to face with a stalking Daogankpa, she stood still for a second, but then broke the stillness of the situation with a very wide smile. The dog began to bark, and had to be restrained with a tug on his leash. Daogankpa feared that he was about to piss, standing right in front of this fairy, when she surprised him again by greeting him in his language. All he could do at that moment was return a half-baked smile, a blob of a response and dash back to the trail that had led him to this strange moment of time in his life.

On the day of the bull chase, Daogankpa had mixed emotions. For one, he was nervous about losing. He simply had to be the one to break the chain of defeat for his *morung*. This bull was the biggest he had ever seen. To exacerbate all such worries, he was told by someone that the Memsahab, along with her entourage of servants, would be watching the race. He struggled to focus on his mission as flashes of the brief and awkward encounter with the Memsahab only a few weeks ago kept intruding on his thoughts. He had dreamt of her almost every other day since. It was a good thing that people often find the memories of their dreams slipping away soon after awakening, for the contents of Daogankpa's dreams involving the Memsahab were best left forgotten. As people from his rival *morung* started coming into the field, he reclaimed his focus.

The runners were all huddled on the street in groups, signifying the undercurrent of rivalry that was rapidly charging the atmosphere. The usual paraphernalia around the men—cloaks, beads, head ornaments— had all been discarded for loincloths. They were from rival *morungs* from within and outside Laisong village. Their patrons made sure that their representatives had been amply fortified with rituals, ceremonies and of course, rice beer. The air reeked of tension from the impending competition. The streets were deserted, with children locked inside their homes and only a few undaunted women seen peering from behind half-opened doors and windows. The dangers were known to all, as were the simple rules of the game. The first ones to catch the bull and throw it to the ground would be declared victors. If only it were this simple. The chase and the final showdown with the bull involved not only a near-fatal struggle with the beast, but also a tough fight with the rivals from the participating *morungs* for final supremacy.

Kicks, slaps, bites and punches during the game were known to leave lasting scars on the *morung* boys. Deogankpa's own father had lost an eye during his time. He had passed the remainder of his days in the village as a hero of his *morung* until his death. As per custom, the village priest and his assistant were to herald the start of the grand chase. As the assistant cut the bull's tether with a hard swing of his *dao,* the village priest inflicted an almost visible blow onto the bull's rump with a stout, decorated stick, making the bull dash away as fast as possible from that sharp, unpleasant sensation. And so the chase began.

It was an astonishing sight. A thundering bull running helter-skelter about narrow village lanes, throwing off any and everything in its way. From wood stacks to haystacks, to water pipes and the flood of men chasing after it with fierce determination and wild self-belief. After about fifteen minutes or so, the bull trampled through a few homesteads and gardens and vanished into the woods, with the file of bellicose men behind its trail. Deogangkpa was somewhere in the middle of this file. Despite fatigue forming a giant claw in his chest and choking him from within, he kept reminding himself that it wasn't about the speed, it was the strategy. He was relying on conserving his strength by keeping a steady pace which could potentially bubble into a burst of strength that he would most definitely need at the very last moment to restrain the bull. Stamina and strength had to go hand in hand.

While on the chase, his only concern was to not lose sight of the bull's rear; he didn't need to increase his speed until he found the bull trapped in a spot of narrow to no escape. From the corner of his eye, he could see his rivals storm past him with lightning speed, many of whom he encountered panting and gasping on the ground only a few minutes later. But he stayed steady. In a short while, he found himself alone on the chase, his rivals not within his peripheral vision. Finding himself in a gully, he suddenly heard some shouting coming from the far bank and instinctively ran towards it, legs quickening on their own accord. When he met the source of the sound, he was dumbfounded by the scene before his eyes.

The bull was stationary. A few paces away from it was the Memsahab and her servant Namkia, frozen still. Deogankpa looked from the Memsahab to the bull and back again. Her eyes caught his for a brief second. His breath stopped; he didn't know whether it was from the sheer novelty of the sight or the lack of fear in her eyes. It was almost as if she was preparing to crouch, and her stillness was only a momentary stance before she would pounce on the beast herself. After what seemed like mere seconds but also an entire lifetime of waiting, Deogankpa launched himself at the bull with all his might, catching its tail with both his hands, his feet digging into the ground beneath as the bull prepared for a feral flight.

Deogankpa's world began to spin, and he felt his feet flying above the ground, his body hurled into the air. Soon after, another pair of hands caught hold of the tail and roars from both man and beast filled the air. Before he knew it, the number of hands grew around the body of the beast and it was thrown to the ground. Deogankpa had fallen flat on his face himself, his arms numb, but clutching the coveted tail.

At last, victory to his *morung*. The mood in the dormitory was most jovial and rice beer was flowing like a perennial river. Deogankpa was flung in the air yet again, this time by his celebrating comrades, who weren't gentle around his bruised body. His right arm was particularly hurt, skinned and bleeding. Deogankpa did not mind. His inebriated self was far too elated to feel any pain. Not only had he brought prestige to his *morung*, but he had also etched a name for himself in the Memsahab's mind. He had saved her life after all.

Apparently, curiosity had got the better of her once the chase had begun, and she had coaxed a reluctant Namkia to follow the noises she could hear. Hoping that it meant the arrest of the bull, she had ventured deep into the woods to capture the scene on her metal box, which the village now knew to be a 'camera'. What was most astounding for Deogankpa was the stance his Memsahab had taken, devoid of fear, with eyes almost as savage as the beast itself. He had never seen or known anyone like her before. He was madly in love.

'Whatever in the world is going to happen to us Zeme people? We are neither British nor Japanese. Why should we get pulled into their wars?' The first councillor spoke up.

The heads of the neighbouring Zeme Naga villages were having an emergency meeting at Laisong after hearing very disturbing news only a day before. Their beloved Memsahab was being ordered by the British administration to travel to Lumding, a four-day trek from Laisong, to run a canteen for the refugees fleeing the Japanese attack in Burma. They were informed by some Zeme brothers who worked at the government offices in Halflong town that the Japanese had dropped bombs on some ships that belonged to the great nation of America. Now the world was embroiled in a nasty war and the British Empire was at quite the centre of things. Japan was at loggerheads with Britain. Apparently, the nation of Japan was not very far from Assam and as the region was part of British India, a plan to invade it was underway.

'When will we Zemes find peace? First the Kacharis, then the British, and now possibly the Japanese! Maybe they will come to our villages looking for enemies. The Memsahab is British. Let us not forget this.' A councillor who was of a paranoid disposition in general and suspicious of Ursula in particular made the statement, with no effort to conceal his sardonic tone.

A buzz spread through the crowd, interrupted by another councillor, who was one of the beneficiaries of the colonial administration as three of his sons worked clerical jobs in

Haflong at the district headquarters. 'See, my brothers. It has been a hundred years since we began cultivating under the British. They have given us protection from raids, given us roads and salt-markets. Must we not side with them in this great war of theirs?'

A silence ensued.

'I encourage all esteemed members present here to not lose sight of why we have all gathered here today. This is not a deliberation about any war. This is not a debate on choosing sides, for when the time comes, if it comes, we know that the Japanese will hack us with no thought nor mercy. We are here to find a solution for our beloved Memsahab who is burdened with a task too heavy even for men. She has made our village her homeland and we must do what we can to help her in times of despair.' The councillor from Laisong offered his opinion.

The paranoid councillor countered this opinion by stating that perhaps it was the Memsahab's own doing. She must have desired this. After all, it was the Empire's blood that flowed through her veins, not a Naga's.

The Laisong councillor was not having this. He urged the gathering to recall how she treated them and their families with medicines, taking care of the sick and ailing with the help of her Zeme servants. She was not part of the offices in Haflong and was living in harmony with the Zeme people for years now, partaking in their culture and traditions. Did this not make her one of their own? Unlike the other British people who had come to live among them with an agenda of condemning their Gods and their way of life, Uu-su-la Memsahab was doing no such thing. Maybe the British had stopped seeing her as their own and were hence pushing her towards a precarious situation. But that was not the Zeme way of doing things. They took care of their own and it was time they extended this care to the Memsahab.

This monologue found support amongst the majority in the gathering. With a collective consensus about the Memsahab needing their protection, they decided to visit the district headquarter in Haflong and petition before Sub-Divisional Officer, Sir Perry, to undo the unfair order. The paranoid councillor quietly slipped away from the crowd and made for his village with no one noticing.

Several opposing thoughts and feelings were nibbling at Henry Perry's mind like parasites, unsettling him acutely. This, he could not afford. This loosening of the threads holding him together had to be contained; he was, after all, a civil servant of the greatest empire known to mankind. An empire that stood on perilous ground at the moment. Their most prized colony was under threat and all the rest had been upended by the

Second World War. However, Churchill was not one to relent. He set their priorities straight for the nation, proclaiming *status quo ante helium* as the primary aim during the War. Colonies had to remain colonies. Whether it was the 'crown jewel' India or tactical Burma. The war had to be fought assiduously; if not for the principal of righteousness, then for defending hard-earned possessions, a habit cultivated through centuries of colonial craftsmanship.

The Empire was facing the most challenging of times they had since Napoleon. This was Perry's personal belief. He knew even before the war broke out that the lofty leaders of the great Occident would fail to circumvent conflict. Even after the ghastly ramifications of the First World War, conditions to pull the world back into the hellish clutches of a second war kept being created. And ironically, he, an archeology enthusiast from the alluring city of Bath, was a core constituent in this global mess.

His posting as Sub-Divisional Officer in the North Cachar Hills of Assam Province was his third assignment after joining the Indian Civil Services. He had managed to conceal his reservations about joining the service quite well from his proud, retired civil servant of a father. But never had he imagined that these reservations and doubts would resurface this early on in his career. While there was no denying that he thoroughly enjoyed certain parts of his profession, especially the opportunity afforded to him to closely interact with the most fascinating races known to mankind, the context that created these opportunities could very well be questioned. And he certainly was.

Was it indeed the white man's burden to introduce a notion of civilisation so tethered to the Occident, to the Empire, upon a people that pirouetted around an entirely different sun? Or was it wiser for their supposedly advanced civilisation to let the Orient rotate on its own axis? In recent times, Perry had found himself gravitating towards the latter stream of thought which was, despite all his resistance, beginning to germinate within his very mind and heart as a core belief. He blamed the Nagas in his constituency for this.

Never before in his life had he encountered a people so intriguing, visceral and ineradicable from the natural landscape to which they harnessed their souls. Perry was riveted by all that concerned the Nagas—from their elusive genesis and migration to this part of the world to their wildly exotic features, from their customs and rituals to their ability to branch and diverge into sub-tribes but continue to draw life from a seemingly integrated umbilical cord of shared heritage.

In his admiration of the Nagas, their heinous savageries had to be added into the bargain too. During the early days of his posting in Halflong, he went on far too many exploration visits to better acquaint himself with his new surroundings. It was on one of these visits that his guide, whether by sinister choice or sincerity of intent, took him to the hut of an erstwhile headhunter. Perry was not prepared. All four walls of the mud-plastered hut displayed the grotesque visages of severed heads which had fallen victim to a preposterous lust for power; the more heads in one's basket, the better was their shot at leadership. Perry had to dash out of the hut to prevent a public regurgitation, for the visit of the Sahab merited nearly the whole village to gather where he stood. Yet, Perry had always been inclined to make corroborations, to draw logical deductions about the past and the present. Europe, too, had gone through its fair share of decapitations, skinning, mutilations and arson. It was the way of the world. It was the way of man.

It was 1944 now, five years since the war had broken out and although Perry had felt greatly distanced from the menacing affray for the larger part of the war, he could now hear the bomb ticking right next to his ears. The Japanese were already in Kohima, approximately 250 km from Haflong. They were being held out by a British battalion and some additional garrison troops. Perry was as alert as a hawk. He kept close contact with the corresponding units that provided near-daily information on both Kohima and Imphal.

At Imphal, a large perimeter had been established, with the allied troops defending the surrounding heights. Like most other British personnel in India, Perry was deeply aware that the present problem was not solely related to the Japs. The fast-deteriorating domestic situation was another major caustic factor. The Indian National Congress was covertly reaping the best out of a war-torn world order while one of their own took several giant leaps outside the country and joined forces with the Axis camp. It was beyond Perry's comprehension how Bose was leading his Indian National Army on the eastern front under a Japanese command. Indeed, was it time for the Empire to recalibrate its relationship with the colonies? The part of Perry that deepened his inner turmoil and conflict believed so.

Compounding his confusion was Miss Ursula Graham Bower, although he had to admit that this confusion was far from the pessimistic kind. He was thoroughly enthralled by her situation. A young British woman who had left the cozy comforts of home to spend years of her life with not just any other Indian populace, but the Nagas, assimilating with their mysteries and blatancies. He could hardly forget the day when a group of Naga village headmen had hounded his office, protesting the government's orders for her to manage a canteen for the inbound refugees from Burma. How could he possibly convince them of their *daughter's* enthusiasm over the order? They could be satisfied only with strong reassurances by Perry that he would personally see to her safety and get her back to them safe and sound. How wonderfully strange human bonds were!

For Perry, Miss Bower was many things at once. A keen student, ardent explorer, diligent researcher, promising anthropologist, talented documenter, lover of peril and guns, and above all, a real humanist. With the onset of the war, this 'Naga Queen', as she was now known amongst the British circuit, had been approached with a unique proposition—to create a guerilla unit with her Naga brethren, the Watch and Ward, to monitor enemy infiltration.

Never in a hundred years could Perry have anticipated such an arrangement for a British memsahab. And boy, did she do justice to it! Many a times, it was Miss Bower who kept Perry's motivation afloat, with her meticulous study of maps and enemy lines. Her command as a woman far exceeded that of several hot-blooded Briton males and to convince her to taper down was only an exercise in futility.

Perry could hardly forget when Memsahab Perry had once invited the newly arrived Memsahab Bower for dinner at their bungalow. The juxtaposition between the two interacting women could hardly go amiss amidst the curious invitees, much to the amusement of Perry. Instead of a discussion about how taffeta and Chinese silk were thoroughly unsuited to the Assamese weather, Miss Bower was more inclined towards discussing boar-hunting schedules with the room.

It was now known far beyond Assam, right up to the gentrified palatial halls of Calcutta, that there resided amongst the Nagas of the East, a wondrous creature from the soils of Britain who was best suited to be referred to as a 'Jungle Queen' rather than a memsahab. Wherever she moved, her entourage of Nagas would move alongside her. They were one rank, one file and this was the aspect that led Perry to often ponder; what was she? A loyal subject of the Empire, flinging herself to the service of her nation in the most hostile and difficult of regions out there, against an invading eastern army? Or was she indeed a 'Naga Queen', a daughter of the people of this strange, alien land, whose consciousness had entwined itself with hers, whether knowingly or unknowingly. Was she, as Perry often found himself wondering, a false friend or a true foe?

Sunsets in the East (1962)

The stench was inside her house now. It was not just her prayer mates from the *namghar*;[1] several neighbours had started complaining about it as well. Ever since the Dalai Lama had descended to the Assam Valley from Lhasa three years ago, on the way to his palace of exile, his Lamas had been following suit. Perhaps, mused Rupohi, one needn't shower every day in extremely cold places like Tibet. But Lord Krishna knew, in a place like Tezpur, nestled in the hot and humid valley of Assam, even autumn was a mild furnace.

The *namghar,* whose keepers had been kind enough to host a few monks, was a few houses away from her own. The Lama camp in Missamari, just on the outskirts of Tezpur town, had flooded beyond its capacity with Tibetan exiles. So much so that people around town, including religious establishments such as her *namghar,* had offered up their spaces to them. Was it alright for guests to continue their native habits even

1 A prayer hall for Vaishnavites

when in exile? Shouldn't the most basic practices of their host community (such as daily baths) be followed?

'Krishna, Krishna,' sighed Rupohi, removing her handkerchief from her nose, slowly moving her heavy, arthritis-ridden legs away from the verandah towards the corridor. Her spine—curved dramatically to the left by scoliosis—and her heavy, swollen ankles impeded her mobility. In her case though, such debilitation of the physique was far outrun by a sharp mind and an even sharper tongue. It was in her ancestral village, a few miles outside Tezpur, that she had earned the epithet of *donduri*. This title carried itself with her to her brother's town, Tezpur, where she had shifted many years ago.

Donduri, or ever-quarrelsome Rupohi, picked fights with all and sundry, from her own family to their neighbours and sometimes, total strangers. Standing four feet and ten inches tall; pudgy and ebony-skinned, tongue eternally stained orange with incessant betel-chewing; she would often hear people jeering, 'Look, Ma Kali is here for a duel,' alluding to Goddess Kali's blood-red tongue, except Rupohi was considered the opposite of a vanquisher of evil. Anything could provoke her. A wailing infant, a shopkeeper's lack of change, directionless travellers, extremely thorny fish, croaking toads and playful children were only a few of Rupohi's pet peeves.

Perennially detached from all humans, the only thing that grounded her was the *namghar*, the community prayer house, to which she was completely devoted. She wouldn't miss a single day of congregational prayers and her hymn-singing mates at the establishment were possibly the only set of people she couldn't get offended by, although not for lack of trying. She had fully submitted to Lord Krishna but often wondered how his love extended to the imbeciles that surrounded her at all times. Someday, when she reunited with her Supreme Lord, she would ask him that.

At present, her cause of ire was her vapid, dim-witted niece who still hadn't brought her the betel leaf and nut she had asked for a long time ago.

'Poornima! Is it done or not? How long must an old lady wait for her *paan*? Must this century get over before you finish a simple task?' Rupohi was yelling now, limping along the never-ending corridor into the kitchen where Poorima was supposed to be.

'Is this nuisance necessary at nine in the morning? Witches rise early it seems, only to make people's ears bleed,' her nephew Arup shot back. For him, a tussle a day with his father's sister was as ritualistic as community prayers.

'What nuisance? I am simply calling out your spoilt sister, who can't do a single thing on time! Lord knows which good family will ever ask for her hand at this rate. Seventeen already, talentless and without suitors. No surprises there.' Rupohi snapped back with habitual contempt.

Crash! came the sound of something shattering.

Even before Rupohi had finished her sentence, Arup hurled his tea cup to the floor and dashed to the kitchen, looking for his sister. A frail-looking Poornima was caught off-guard and stumbled on her *mekhela*, her waist-long braid swinging like a pendulum as her older brother pulled her out of the kitchen by her arm and brought her before their aunt.

Arup stood in front of his sister; a lion by its cub. With unnatural calmness, he faced his aunt and said, 'Listen closely, once and for all. First, you are no old woman. Nowhere in human history is forty-five regarded old enough for the kind of tantrums you throw. Second, Poornima is not your servant, unlike Ma, whom you made sure to turn into one, and finally murder.'

In the same breath, he turned towards Poornima and asked, 'And you, what are you even doing here at this hour? Shouldn't you be in school already?' Poornima kept her timid stare fixed on the floor, her long braid now still, like a glistening black snake at rest. A heavy stillness consumed the space between Arup, Poornima and Ruphohi.

'You ungrateful brats!' spat Rupohi, puncturing that stillness that had survived no less than thirty seconds. 'Who are you calling a murderer, you ingrate! When your mother died, it was I who…'

The sound of what would have been a savage retaliation drowned as Arup made his way out of the house, making sure to grab Poornima's school bag as he left, fully aware of the pointlessness of going to a mostly deserted school.

Ramen Sharma felt quite disengaged from work that day. The year 1962 was getting scarier by the day, with reminders constantly afloat in a place like the Deputy Commissioner's office where he worked as a clerk. It was one thing to be bombarded with news about the escalating border tensions with China through the newspapers and radio. Within the confines of paper and a transistor box, such things seemed far away, as they should be. But when military strategists started mushrooming in every corner of the office, even the sweeper's arena, things appeared to be uncomfortably close. He was often reprimanded by his co-workers for his lack of participation in such discussions.

'Uff Ramen *da*! Think! What will happen if the Chinese cross the North-East Frontier Agency (NEFA) and make their way down to the Assam valley? You do realise that Tezpur will be the first victim of their eastern conquest, right? I have heard that they don't even spare dead babies, and stew them along with the rats. Can you fathom in your wildest dreams what will become of us under the control of such hellhounds?' His colleague Dhiraj had lamented a couple of days before.

Little did Dhiraj know that his words had sent a chill down Ramen's spine, a chill he had been experiencing intermittently, starting from the aftermath of his wife Rina's death two years ago. The chills were more frequent now, making unwelcome appearances during Rupohi and Arup's violent arguments, or when he helplessly watched his daughter's household burdens piling up. Or whenever the word 'war' came up.

Since July, the situation had been rapidly deteriorating, with the Chinese mobilising themselves stealthily around the McMahon line while augmenting their ammunitions stockpile in occupied Tibet. Just the previous month, in September, after a confirmed Chinese presence on both banks of the Namkha Chu valley well within the NEFA, a skirmish between Indian and Chinese soldiers had led to casualties on both sides. Things were almost at their doorstep now. Ramen, who had battled anxiety throughout his life, was already losing sleep over these distressing developments. Why wouldn't he? With the Home Guards for Civil Defence starting to train Tezpur's women to handle guns, Chinese aggression no longer seemed like a fable from the borders. Ramen could visualise a dark and sinister tornado uprooting everything on its pathway, a spiral of death and destruction ready to consume all and sundry, especially his beloved

Tezpur, a town which could be reached by the red tornado in less than a day's journey from the NEFA.

War talks, particularly war-time strategies, were too confusing for Ramen to process. If a full-scale war was imminent, why had the Chinese premier visited New Delhi just the previous day, announcing his resolve to settle the disputes diplomatically? As if these perplexing messages weren't enough, his home town currently abounded with war symbols. Supply-laden military trucks were a common sighting, making people morbidly insecure about what was to come. Perhaps in response, 'vigilant groups' had sprouted across town to keep an all-night vigil lest they all get stumped by the Chinese in their sleep. Many young men, such as his 21-year-old son, had voluntarily joined the Youth Emergency Organization (YEO), whose members had pledged all kinds of support to ease the burden on the Indian army. One day, it was clearing the roadway from the Balipara to Missamari army camp for better load movement; the next, they were paying home visits to ask for donations for the National Defence Fund.

Legions of tribes from the adjoining NEFA areas had started seeking refuge amidst their valley brethren. The Apatanis, Mishmis, Monpas and many others were a common sight, ambling into Tezpur with their children, cattle and cooking pots, all dangling in clusters, their eyes wandering yet stagnant. Contributions of food, money and shelter had been generously offered by the townsmen to these wanderers who seemed like refugees in their own country.

Worse still was the thinning population of the town itself, with people steadily slipping out elsewhere. Schools and colleges resembled leisure grounds more than learning centres. The town felt like a slow-dripping water tap.

Transformations like these were always complicated. Even more so for someone like Ramen, who always aimed for the shore, the safety of a destination. For as long as he could remember, a calm and stable life was all he had ever wished for. Never one to take extreme positions or stands, he preferred adorning *swadeshi* without burning British goods. Just as he welcomed India's independence from the periphery rather than joining the suicide squads in Tezpur during the freedom struggles.

Nonetheless, calm evaded him. Especially in his own home, ever since Rupohi became his sole responsibility after his parents' death. As the eldest son in the family, it naturally fell upon him to take in his unmarried, handicapped sister. But in truth, the weight was fully borne by his wife Rina. From silently receiving Rupohi's compulsive criticisms to religiously slicing betel nuts in the exact measure of her sister-in-law's preferences, Rina took care of each one of Rupohi's needs, even if that meant giving her space to spill her bile.

Other than slight reprimands, Ramen had preferred to look away rather than properly confront, being the eternal pacifist. Deep within him had lurked a terrible sense of sadness; on one hand, for his inability to cure or even reduce his sister's malady and on the other, his inability to ease Rina's crushing burdens. Perhaps Rina understood this, or had simply accepted her husband's lack of gumption, and hence had never tried to fight the overbearing third-party presence in her home.

But then there was Arup. Extremely attached to Rina, he found ways to retaliate against Rupohi as his father failed to. As a young boy, he came to his mother's aid by adding chilli powder to Rupohi's tea or hiding toads under her pillow. Even as a ten-year-old, he knew his father's passive acceptance of his aunt's impropriety somehow extended to him too. He would certainly get a smack or two from his mother for his pranks, but he was aware of the special love his parents had for him. He had often caught snippets of conversations about how he was a latecomer in this world. He had arrived after two goat sacrifices, six planetary alignment *pujas* and hundreds of rupees spent in donations to Brahmins, in the seventh year of his parents' marriage. Fortified by this knowledge, Arup was sure that he would not be easily abandoned by his family. And so he nurtured his wrath for Rupohi undeterred.

Rupohi, on the other hand, found fault in every inch of her nephew, from the way he chewed his food to the way he spoke. She attributed most mishaps in the household to his impish presence, making no pretense to conceal her disdain for him. The fire burnt both ways. By the time of Rina's death, Arup's pranks had transformed to scathing verbal attacks against the woman he held solely responsible for his mother's failing health. For Arup, the tumour that ate away his mother's brain was birthed by Rupohi's disapprovals and denunciations. He would often prefix his sentences with 'You witch!' before hurling them at Rupohi while he was growing up. At the present moment, 'witch', has been replaced with, 'insane', 'deranged', 'evil' and sometimes, 'parasite'.

Thus, for Ramen, a sense of calm had made only rare appearances in his life. Now with an impending Chinese invasion, his universe seemed anything but safe and stable. Both inside and outside his home.

'*Deuta*,[2] we have not really made proper contributions to the war effort. I know we are not in a cushy situation at the moment, but there must be something we can contribute.' Arup coaxed his father on an insipid October afternoon.

Ramen was lounging on what used to be his father's chair, the frame too big for his slight stature. He resembled a

2 *Deuta* means 'father' in Assamese

middle-school boy in adult clothing; bearded, trying to read the newspaper with overly thick spectacles.

'Hmmm, you are right about our situation, but do you have a suggestion in mind?' replied Ramen, purposely modulating his tone in a way that conveyed empathy without necessarily fanning the hopes of the listener. This was his go-to style with his family.

'I was thinking...maybe now that Ma is no longer with us, her wedding jewellery could be put to the highest, most virtuous use,' responded Arup with calculated pauses, his nerves tingling. Arup knew that he *ought to* love his father, for this was a blood bond. But years of the patriarch's timidity before Rupohi had eroded any feelings of love or respect he might have had, leaving only the wisdom to not antagonise his father the way he did his despicable aunt.

On hearing his son's suggestion, Ramen cleared his throat, all the while keeping his eyes focused on the newspaper he had finished reading a long time ago. '*Beta*, jewellery and everything is quite a feminine business. Only women know the most appropriate use for all that, especially considering that your sister is yet to get married. But I understand your point and I want to support you. Your mother's belongings are not in my custody. Maybe you can ask your aunt.' Ramen crafted this response very carefully, adding Poornima mid-sentence, hoping it would offset the potentially dangerous conclusion.

To Ramen's utter surprise, his son was not instantly riled up by this and instead, walked calmly to the verandah where Rupohi sat peeling garlic. With deliberate politeness, he asked, '*Pehi*,[3] can you tell me where you have kept Ma's wedding jewellery?'

Rupohi's garlic-peeling became slightly aggressive. Without looking at her nephew, she replied, 'Why do you need to know the whereabouts of your mother's jewellery? It is safe and shall be kept in this family for important occasions.'

Arup stood silent for a second and with exercised patience, spoke again. 'I need to know where it is, so I can donate at least some of it, if not all, towards the war effort. This *is* an important occasion. Probably the most important one we will see in our lifetimes. So please cooperate, not just with me, but with our nation, and release them from your watch,' he concluded as calmly as was humanly possible for him.

At this, Rupohi turned her twisted body towards him, along with the full force of her wrath, and snapped, 'Release from my watch? My watch! What do you think I am? Your family's guard dog? And why should I do that? For crooked *netas* and phony leaders? One day it is *Hindi-Chini Bhai Bhai*. The next day at each other's throats! How do you know for sure where all this donated gold and money will go? I trust no one. Let the Chinese come and butcher me. At least I will be free

3 *Pehi* means 'aunt' in Assamese

from this miserable house.' Her tirade pulled Ramen out of his chair and he stood transfixed by the door of the verandah, a few steps behind Arup on purpose.

'You deranged, selfish woman!' roared Arup this time, his self-restraint finally coming undone. 'Do you have an inkling of what will happen if the Chinese invade us? You want to die, "find freedom from this miserable house" as you call it, be my guest. Offer yourself up like the goat you are. But what about the rest of us? Do you want to see Poornima get raped in front of the whole town, or see your brother's throat slit open? I know you wish to see me hanged with barbed wire, but what about your own community, the *namghar*, your prayer mates? WHAT ABOUT THEM, YOU WIT—'

'Arup! Enough.' He was interrupted by Ramen. At this, Arup turned towards his father and blurted out, 'NOW, you choose to speak up? What in the world is wrong with you, *Deuta*! For as long as I remember, you have stood by this woman and watched as she destroyed Ma, and now us. You couldn't man up for your wife and protect her as she swept, mopped, fixed and fed with a tumour in her brain while your sister sat chewing her betel leaf and picking on her.'

Ramen tried to speak but Arup was not done.

'I will never understand your reverence for this dangerous snake you keep around you, around us.' He continued, 'She wants to keep Ma's belongings to herself, just as she has done with most things in this house, including you, all to feed her bottomless ego. And I for one, will no longer be witness to this. Let me know when she is finally out of here.'

With this, he dashed to his room and started packing, making quick plans to stay with a YEO friend for a while. Poornima trotted behind him like a pony and pleaded with her brother, '*Dada*, why so much anger? Please don't do this. You can't leave me this way.'

Arup didn't look up, as he knew that the anger flowing through his veins would ensure that he followed through with his plan. Seeing his now-weeping sister would be an unwelcome breach. He quickly packed up the frugal belongings he had and walked out of his house, with these words to his sister: 'Take care of our foolish father.'

'Tawang has fallen! They are approaching! Emergency declared!' bawled Rupam, the YEO General Secretary, panting heavily as he rushed into the room where Arup and a few others were discussing their work distribution. With the onset of full-fledged fighting between the two countries since October 20th, the YEO members had been seen running about in every nook and corner of the town. From increasing self-defence training over the last six days in collaboration with the police to facilitating the supply of goods to the military base camp, YEO members had joined the scene at full throttle. Moments before Rupam's dramatic entrance, Arup and his compatriots had been chalking out a plan to search for rejected elderly citizens dumped in trenches dug on family compounds by escaping family members. Four such cases had been reported in the last five days. A massive exodus had begun.

'Where did you hear this?' A fellow member asked Rupam.

'A public announcement was blaring on the streets! I was just leaving home but I ran back in to grab the transistor so we can all hear,' replied Rupam. Coming from generational wealth and tea money, he belonged to a family that could afford a personal radio. Around a dozen of them were huddled around this curious box that could speak. The words spoken in this instance, however, evoked the worst of emotions; anxiety, anger, fear, shame, and to some degree, a sense of hopelessness.

'I knew this would happen!' burst out Pulok.

'How much more can be expected from an undersupplied army? We can count our doom on our fingertips now. Remind me, brothers, Tawang is, what, three to four hundred kilometres away? They might get here anytime now. What's with the absence of the Airforce even now! Do we all have to be charred by the Red Dragon, every man, woman and child, before airstrikes are ordered? Or is Nehru expecting us to welcome them with marigold garlands and Assam tea?'

Everyone was quiet as they knew that the points raised by haughty Pulok had weight, but no one had any valid responses to them.

'Listen, Pulok, even with the full support of our Airforce, we aren't sure we can tilt the scales totally in our favour, given the sheer force of Chinese deployment. We can probably only delay movement. So I strongly suggest we focus on what we can do now on the ground, in Tezpur, to safeguard our people rather than worry about the war outcome,' this was humbly put forth by Tarun, a primary school teacher, his patiently delivered opinion reflecting his suitability for his profession.

'But Tarun *da*, imagine standing against an avalanche of bloodthirsty Chinese soldiers in that bitter, bitter cold with the kind of uniforms our soldiers have. And with what? A few donated rifles from the police? Catapults and *daos*? Call me a cynic but since Independence, have we not concentrated maximum resources and vigilance over the western border? What about the East?' Pulok's spite only seemed to be strengthening.

Finally, Arup stepped in to realign their focus, which was all they could afford to do at the moment. 'Pulok, calm down,' he added with a firmer tone.

'As Tarun *da* mentioned and I am sure we can all agree on—we cannot afford to lose any time in theories and debates on what should have been and what isn't. God forbid, if a day arrives when we have to meet with the enemy even with a sickle in our hands, we will just have to go through with it. Let's get down to business and streamline our duties quickly, starting with the roster for the night watch.'

'Ramen *Khura...khura*, are you there?'

A frantic thumping on Ramen's main door startled all three members of the household. They had been cooped up inside their house for weeks now. Ramen had stopped going to work after the Emergency had been declared. Not that anyone had noticed his absence, given the mayhem in Tezpur since the outbreak of the Sino-Indian war.

In the evenings, the colony shape-shifted into a graveyard, the resemblance deepening with the blackout. Congregational songs from the *namghar* stopped entering their homes with the evening breeze. Oil lanterns hung from porches like ignored carcasses, lest the glow attract unwarranted attention. Crossing over to the other side of the Brahmaputra on steamboats was the new ritual, pursued mechanically by the townspeople as an act of survival. For those who chose to stay behind, each passing day was like a divine gift. The remaining few people in Tezpur felt like the fish in the shallow water-drums at the fish market, about to be picked unto their death at any second; each gulp of air a challenge to their inevitable fate.

Ramen went to answer the door only because the dusk afforded some safe light. Yusuf, his neighbour's son, stood on the other side of it. A bit younger than Arup, he was double his height, or that of anyone in the colony, towering at about six feet and three inches. On seeing Ramen, Yusuf started, a little out of breath as he spoke, '*Khura,* Bomdila has been taken. Word is, they are closing in on Missamari. The army stationed there has started getting rid of the ammunitions. I have been on the night watch since yesterday and was told to visit each house in the vicinity to find people and see if they need safe passage to the river bank. A steamer leaves in about an hour, *khura*. Are you ready? *Khura*? Ramen *Khura*!'

Ramen departed to another dimension as Yusuf spoke, the boy's words sounding like gibberish. His hands began shaking with a little more violence than he preferred and it was only when Rupohi appeared by his side that he returned to his body.

'What happened, boy, why are you here?' Rupohi asked the colossal figure before her.

When she heard his news, she rejected him outright and said, 'I am not leaving my home, let them come. If I go to the Lord's abode, I will take the first steps from my *namghar*. Although I am sure those rascals will melt on setting foot in this neighbourhood. Such is the power of my *namghar*.'

Not knowing how to respond and also aware of the futility of an argument with the infamous Rupohi, Yusuf turned to Ramen and said, '*Khura*, time is running out and I have to cover this whole area. Please hurry and leave, I am sorry but I have to go now.' He was already half-jumping on his bicycle as he said these words.

Ramen's mind, heart and eyes ached in synchrony. For Arup.

With the fall of Bomdila, only 150 km away, Tezpur's transition to a ghost town was nearly complete. The last coherent sound around the town was the sombre radio voice of the Prime Minister expressing his sympathy for the people of Assam at their misfortune. *My heart goes out to the people of Assam at this hour.*

To a lot many listeners in Tezpur, those words signaled their forsaken fates. Hence, many of them began running 'errands' to defer fate, if not defeat it. While the state bank's manager made the farsighted choice of burning currency notes and dumping coins in a local pond, the famous hospital for the mentally infirm released some of the 'better off' patients. Some of the freed inmates must have attributed their sudden freedom to either divine intervention or to the Chinese, as a few walked around the deserted streets of Tezpur chanting *China zindabaad!* No consequences for such crimes of treason, as the figureheads of civil administration and police were all gone.

Somewhere. Anywhere but a town so doomed. The mighty river, too, witnessed a strange scene by its north bank as a crowd of people, regardless of their social status, stood, sat, or squatted, waiting for the steamboats. Terror has been known to be a great equaliser.

Arup was at the riverbank. He was running from person to person, asking if they were thirsty or hungry, while his father's and sister's faces showed up in front of his eyes intermittently. Even amidst the havoc, he could sense his own bewilderment as the silhouette of Rupohi kept itself stationed in every mental frame that held his family. While his mind's eye fought a battle, the other pair rummaged through the crowd. At one point, they were drawn to a rock, a little over a metre from where Arup was standing. A half-asleep figure was laid against the rock, another kneeling beside it, weeping wildly. A toddler was clinging to its arm. Both the sleeping and weeping figures seemed young, not much older than Arup himself. When Arup reached close enough, armed with water and bread, his feet stopped working. The half-asleep figure by the rock was as still as the rock itself, eyes wide open and mouth slightly parted.

Her *mekhela* was soaked in blood, hiding an obstinate cord that clung to its companion, now cold, still and lifeless. Its father wailed, kneeling beside the dead mother. The would-be sibling, meanwhile, sucked on her own fist.

Darkness had fully descended. The eerie silence of the neighbourhood that Ramen, Rupohi and Poornima were getting accustomed to was punctured by distant sounds—exploding, burning, rampaging. It was midnight now, and they were huddled together in one room when suddenly, Poornima heard a soft knock on the kitchen door. The door opened to the backyard of the house. Only one person used that door. Instinctively, she hurried to the kitchen and pressing close to the door, whispered, '*Dada*?'

'Open fast,' Arup responded, to the voice he had missed each day of the entire month he had been away.

When he entered, both sides exercised restraint, lest their voices travel out. Hand in hand, they walked to the room where Ramen and Rupohi sat around an earthen lamp with a juvenile flame latching on to the wick for dear life. No smiles were exchanged, no words spoken as the faint glow of the lamp illuminated Arup's face. He sat down beside Rupohi on the floor, Ramen on her other side. Then very softly, as though the words were an effervescence of the air itself, Rupohi started, 'O Lord, O Narayan. Please forgive all our sins. We submit to your being, if there is no other way for salvation but death. O kind Hari, give us shelter under your feet.' She took her nephew's hand in hers as she continued the unwavering prayer.

Devotional Defiance (1972)

The stage light illuminating his angular face is setting Pradeep on fire. This isn't the first time Pradeep is laying his eyes on Amar. He has encountered the dashing young actor at numerous rehearsals over the past two months and has even stitched the costume Amar now exuberantly displays on stage.

Amar has assumed the gait of his character, a rebel peasant leader stirring nationalistic fervour against the colonialists. How handsome his features are. The face of a male deity made prettier with feminine interruptions, like soft pink lips and long black lashes that curled back to touch the eyelids. The straight, sharp nose; its regal tip visible from the far-left flank of the stage where Pradeep is standing, but too far away for the sea of people seated on the ground with their eyes fixed on the stage.

Pradeep shares the anticipation of the audience. It is his first time watching an official Rupashree Theatre Troupe performance too, and not just a rehearsal. It is mesmerising, the transformative power of stage paraphernalia. How titbits of foam, paint, bamboo, ropes, and the like could come together and create the aura of a space that existed more than a hundred years ago. A hundred and eleven to be precise. About to transpire onstage is a journey to the year 1861, when groups of angry peasants had challenged the British colonialists in a nondescript village called Phulaguri, in the Nagaon district of Assam. This episode came to be regarded as a powerful subaltern uprising against the colonialists and became valourised in modern Assamese memory as the Phulaguri *Dhawa*. As Pradeep watches the first dialogue add life to a memory from a century past, he thanks Lord Krishna with a silent prayer for leading him to where he stands today.

Pradeep is six years old, being pulled through a wave of thrill-seekers, his left hand clutched tightly by his father while the right grips a red pinwheel. His mother and little sister are being rushed towards the open grounds in front of the *satra*, the monastic institution of the Vaishnavites. The monks, firmly devoted to Lord Krishna, choose to express their veneration not merely through verbal prayers but a combination of music, dance and theatre. The manifestation of this is the vibrant *Ankia Naat* or one-act play which serves the dual purpose of shining the divine light of providence not just on the monks but also on devotees outside the monastical order. On this day, Pradeep's family represents some of the many devotees who throng the *satra* field like fireflies glowing with their battery-run torches, searching for the best seats on the ground.

After a tedious search, Pradeep's family end up finding satisfactory seats for themselves, five rows from the stage. While the toddler gets tucked into her mother's lap, Pradeep is squeezed between his father and a stranger. Pradeep despises this arrangement. *He* wants to be tucked in his mother's lap. He knows, however, that any expression of these feelings would only lead to a flaming ear-twisting from his father, if not a slap across his face. He keeps quiet and tries to contain the quivers that form at the corners of his burdened lips.

There are a lot of people on the ground. It is the post-monsoon season, when the skies are clear in Pathshala, a town famous for its cultural contributions to Assam. But the humidity shows itself everywhere as dark, wet patches on people's clothes; a rancid smell floating in the air; weary breaths swallowed laboriously. People seem oblivious to this discomfort, and it nearly dissipates as the benediction begins on stage, invoking divine blessings for what is to come. The stage is simply a raised platform of wooden planks a few inches above the ground. Its precariousness is hardly a concern for its occupants for the night—the musicians, the chief narrator and the actors—all on a mission to serenade their Lord through their individual talents, regardless of how reliable the platform they stand on is.

Pradeep makes an effort to concentrate on what is happening in front of him. After what feels like a long musical night with a singer-musician duo handling percussion instruments and golden cymbals, elaborately dressed men appear onstage with colourful faces, sparkling jewels and thunderous voices. Pradeep doubts whether they are *people* at all, like him or his parents. They resemble the pictures of the gods and goddesses—and even the demons trampled under the feet of those very goddesses—that appear on the paper calendars his mother hangs on their kitchen wall. He cannot comprehend what they are saying as it is all in a language that he does not speak at home with his family or friends. Noticing that somehow, everyone else around him including his own parents, is following the unfamiliar words, he tries to focus too. What carries him away, though, is the strangeness of it all and he cannot help but fixate on the ornate beings before him. The blend of paint on their faces, the bold, dark eyes, the wispy, cloudy hair falling from bejewelled crowns. Everything is embellished, even the swords, *trishuls* and shields.

Even though he is very young, he suspects that the women onstage are actually men. Their voices give them away. The night eventually turns out to be a gala for little Pradeep, until sleep blurs his vision. Whatever remains incomprehensible to him that night starts to unravel and unfold with clarity when year by year, he immerses himself in the ethereal world of theatre, both religious and secular. That night, little Pradeep falls asleep on his father's shoulders with a cloudburst of bright dreams beneath his lids, where he is wearing his favourite red shirt and, twirling with his sister, his face painted like the performers onstage.

Only instead of a sword, he is carrying his red pinwheel as he runs across an open field to nowhere.

Onstage, a group of people are huddled together next to a wavering piece of long blue cloth, signifying a river. Those sitting on the stage floor are the peasants and those elevated atop bamboo shafts are the kings and nobles of the Lalung and Tiwa tribes. They are in intense discussion over the rumoured tax the British are about to impose on betel leaf and nut. What is left for them to tax, they are wondering aloud. Never in their lives before the arrival of these pale leeches had the people paid so much tax. Now they are forced to pay taxes on their total income, for grazing their cattle and even for collecting nature's bounty from the forests! Even worse is the ban on poppy cultivation. Mother

Nature has blessed these people with lands so fertile that poppy oozes out with the ease of weeds. For generations, the people have been growing poppy in homesteads. The wretched British have already infiltrated such spaces, so why can't they stop now? Why continue to spread their vile nets to capture more and more? Are they unaware that the betel leaf and nut are extremely important social symbols for the people? From marriages to worship to death, the betel leaf is as entwined with the lives of the people as it is with the trees that it grows on. No. A line has to be drawn. A unanimous decision is taken in the gathering to visit the Deputy Commissioner's court in Nogaon town and petition their grievances.

Pradeep is eleven. He is unhappy with a few things he has started to notice about his body. Out of nowhere, a few hair strands have appeared around his penis. It is not like the hair he has on his head, which is smooth, straight and long, falling to his ears. His voice has changed.

He hates the sound of it. It is more like his father's than his mother's. He speaks less now, on purpose. He wants to appear as smooth as the blue-eyed doll his sister carries. Not rough to the touch, with the tiny blister-like appearances on his face that he detests. He wishes for his lashes to curl up long and black like that doll's, his lips and cheeks to have that delicious pink tint. It is a toy, he knows. Yet, he envies the smooth triangulation underneath her dress, which he lifts up on a few occasions when no one is looking and touches, to reaffirm the lack of a hideous bulge like his own, with hair spurting out of it now.

What is more different than his body though, is the way his parents are nowadays. It's not like they spoke that much with each other earlier or laughed together in the verandah like his neighbour Jumon's parents. But of late, something has changed even in their minimal levels of conversation. There is a lot of shouting now. Mostly from his once-timid mother. This has been happening since the anklet lady and her toddler visited their house.

He can recall the details of that day with uncanny precision, especially the way she looked, which was unlike anyone he was used to seeing in Pathshala. Coconut-skinned, with not one or two, but *three* nose pins, the third pierced through the septum. The *pallu* of her sari covered her head in a way that not one hair escaped, and the garment was wrapped around her legs in a way that left her ankles exposed. Her ankles were adorned by the most beautifully intricate silver anklets Pradeep had ever seen. That is why, when his mother banished him to his room, he continued peering out from behind a curtain, unable to resist staring at all the silver jewellery on the stranger.

The woman was not loud but seemed to be speaking with conviction, with a babbling toddler around her waist. He couldn't understand much of what was being spoken, firstly due to the distance and secondly due to her using a different dialect. It was only half-familiar to him—a bit of Assamese, a sprinkle of Bengali and several other words in a dense accent. He remembers how his mother turned many shades of red as the woman spoke. She had finally stormed out of the house, screaming out his father's name. Her voice resembled the sounds of the *Bordoisila*, a time before Bihu when the goddess of nature, wind and rain asserted her divination by electrifying the skies with blazing lightening, deafening thunder and torrential downpours that uplifted and uprooted at the same time. His father, who was tending to the kitchen garden at that time, appeared to have lost all the blood in his face at the sight of the strange woman walking slowly towards him behind his briskly advancing wife.

It takes a few years for Pradeep to ascertain everything that had transpired that day. His father, who is a middle-man between farmers and whole-sellers, seemed to be pursuing more than the produce. The woman who had come to Pradeep's house that day was the wife of one of the farmers his father regularly purchased from. But the child with her belonged to

Pradeep's father. She had come to him to ask for money and a one-way ticket to Guwahati where she would take up work as a construction worker. Her husband had apparently thrown her out of her house along with her bastard child. She had walked quite a distance to locate her lover, asking people on the way for directions to the well-known trader's house. Easy to find, it was the first red-brick house right after crossing a famous *namghar.* After his father had hurriedly handed some money to the woman and pushed her out of the house, Pradeep witnessed something for the very first time in his life—his soft-spoken, polite mother screaming 'harami, harami' as she ran behind her husband with a broomstick. A potent weapon, nemesis turned aid. All the while, her husband had shouted back defiantly that the whole thing was a lie, head ducked, hopping around to escape the blows. He had argued that this was a very common allegation faced by those in his line of work so they could be fleeced off of money.

Truth or lie, the episode changes the atmosphere in the household irrevocably. This shift holds a slight advantage for Pradeep. Used to beatings from his father on being found with his sister's dolls or for draping a *sari* and playing house with her, Pradeep seldom receives them after that incident.

Each attack by his father is now countered by his mother with a 'Beat your bastard son, not mine'. Escape has never been certain for Pradeep but it is much easier than it used to be, with his father starting to leave the house for longer stretches than ever before.

'Fast, fast!' A crew member anxiously gestures for Pradeep to change the set background. The ongoing scene depicts a large group of frustrated peasants who have gathered before the Nogaon Deputy Commissioner's office, waiting to meet the Britisher. They are all sitting on the floor of the stage, facing the makeshift façade of a colonial administrative office.

Pradeep and other crew members are to replace the background—blue and green cardboard turns to orange and brown, representing the transition from daylight to dusk. That's how long the peasants had waited for the Deputy Commissioner to lend them an ear, but to no avail. A few seconds after the transition, the melancholic background music gets perforated with the loud, rapturous voices of policemen. *Hatt... jaa... hatt...! Go... Get away from here... get away*, the policemen yell through gritted teeth, wagging their batons for dramatic effect. At this juncture, Amar's character shouts back 'No tax, no foreign rule', as another policeman pulls him away, coaxing him to retreat. Pradeep's throat tightens with clogged desire. Oh, to grab that veined fist challenging the oppressors. But all he can do is take a deep breath and join the ranks of the crew hustling backstage for the next change of scene.

Pradeep is seventeen and has grown quite a bit. He regularly hears comments like 'Shooting up like a betel nut tree, huh!' or 'How much taller will you grow?'. He has gained a few inches indeed, but what is more enticing for Pradeep is how he gets compared to his mother. 'Looking more and more like your mother. You should have been a girl. Would have suited you better.'

Comments like these come to him on more occasions than one, in a variety of tones and phrases. It makes him nervous. Are people in on his secret sojourns to the bathroom where he applies layers of milky cream and turmeric to his face to keep it fair and glowing? Is it obvious that he occasionally steals the baby powder his sister uses to keep his skin looking spot-free? Such things must remain a highly guarded secret so they don't completely upend the composure of his household. His father, who by now is as infrequent a presence in the house as a blue moon, has settled on a working arrangement with his family. Minimum communication, steady contribution. Their house is built on the land given to Pradeep's mother after her marriage by his grandfather, a highly respectable priest in the area. No one in such an arrangement stands to gain from a tumultuous and scandalous household. Pradeep is very aware that his inclinations might lead to just that.

One inclination which he is unable to conceal despite his best efforts is his love for the arts: theatre and cinema. Becoming someone entirely different from who you are and convincing the audience of these false truths is, for Pradeep, a gift, a power. How concocted tales, unreal and inexplicable, can move a person to experience sorrow, rage, wonder, love and longing is a kind of magic. The modern art of filmmaking has him so spellbound that he visits the cinema halls on repeat and sometimes watches up to three films consecutively.

His other obsession is theatre and he usually looks forward to autumn, when monks from the monasteries stage religious plays, the *Ankia Naats*. Unlike the cinema, these are one-act plays and are performed without retakes. When he was younger, they were mostly performed in Brajavali, a medieval poetic language unknown to the common populace. This had kept him from truly immersing himself in the art form. But now, with several *Ankia Naats* happening in Assamese, he can immerse himself in a whole new world replete with dialogue, music, ornaments and idiosyncratic characters. He is convinced that there is nothing like this anywhere in the world. Of late, he has started doing a bit of writing himself, birthing characters, growing them, mutilating them, building another universe where they are as real as the air he breathes.

It is his misfortune that almost everything he loves has to be protected; concealed rather than shared. 'You are either locked in your room with your notebook or wasting your time in cinema halls like a ruffian. When will you start taking interest in your father's business? Who will look after your family?' is his father's oft-repeated admonition for Pradeep.

Over the years, his mother has mostly managed to silence his father in matters of 'disciplining' Pradeep. Yet his father's reprimands sometimes seep through the barricade when it comes to Pradeep's defiant preference for staying locked in his room and writing rather than accompanying his father to the villages for business. Regardless, Pradeep manages to navigate these differences with his father. For him, they are relatively trivial offences compared to what is brewing inside the cattle-shed of his neighbour Jumon's house.

The stage is full. The is the scene where all the actors converge together to depict the *raiz mel*, a gathering where people discussed important matters in their communities during those days. The background is painted with figures of peasants sitting on the ground to create the illusion of how nearly half a thousand of them had gathered during the actual *raiz mel* a century ago.

Onstage, the peasants are having a heated discussion about the apathy of the British sahabs toward their plight.

'What is the point of getting agitated, my friends? We do not wield any power, nor do we simple people understand the ways of the *sarkari* world. If the Deputy Commissioner continues to ignore us, what can we do but remain persistent and keep showing up until he acknowledges us one day?' an old, frail-looking peasant says. The crowd of peasants and their leaders murmur.

'Keep showing up!' Another peasant stands to speak, assuming a commanding position and facing the audience to unleash his monologue. It is Amar. A part of Pradeep stiffens against his will.

'Are we cattle, to keep gathering in places and then getting thrown out? Repeated humiliation is what you are proposing. You have seen how we are treated when we refuse to pay. Have you forgotten how Phaniram was forbidden from the use of his own fields a few months ago? He begged and cried and even kissed the boot of the police. What did he get in return? A broken nose and jaw from the rifle butt. May I remind you who the policeman was? The son of Dhonti *Khura*. *Our* Dhonti from *our* village. Our own kin, our own blood. The white leeches prey not just on our lands but also our people. Turning brother against brother, son against father. We have lost sense of who we are. It is time to get it back!'

He ends on an ecstatic note. The audience claps emphatically. The atmosphere is electric. A few whistles add more spark.

After a brief pause to accommodate the audience's applause, a tribal king speaks up from the bamboo pedestal he is perched on.

'You are correct, my brother. They have attacked our very souls. The souls of our fields, our air, our water. I say this as I have seen strange things happening in my kingdom ever since the white leeches started feeding off of it. Devilish fishes with whiskers, as long and agile as my arm, now live in our fisheries which once were brimming with juicy *rohu* and sweet *pabda*. Pushed out of their own homes, they defy the regime with death and float stiff and cold in unity, sending out a message for us to see. I am sure of it. Last week, a hundred and thirteen black crows were found dead and decaying in the middle of my own poppy fields. The poppy laments, too, for she knows of a change in the tutelage and refuses to yield to anyone but her own people. The scarlet, pulsating poppy now wilts and looks down, beckoning the earth to hold her roots and keep her alive until she finds freedom once again. The earth responds by cracking itself, making room for the poppy to nurture her roots through her own tears.' The actor pauses at this juncture for dramatic effect before unleashing his most practiced line.

'The harmony is lost, my brothers. The *tokari*[1] and *gogona*[2] have stopped listening to one another and play their own tune of discord. '

The poetic monologue fades with a receding melancholic tune in the background. In a few seconds, a leader from a different tribe speaks up.

'Why you lament, I do not understand. If our music has started pouring out sounds of despair, it is because we have allowed others to play us. As for the earth, air and water, they are in fact beckoning us to respond. To answer back and claim what has been taken from us. How dare anyone walk into my kingdom and tell me that I cannot grow my own poppy. I rule by divine right and no one, I repeat, *no one* gets to tax what my kingdom reaps from the land under my divine watch. Yesterday, they laid hands on our poppy, today on our betel nut and leaf, tomorrow, it shall be our women. I for one will not stand and watch this abomination happen. My brothers, our kingdom is getting battle ready and we are training every day. You will find in every nook and corner of my kingdom, the lethal sounds of arrows slicing the air as my

1 *Tokari* is a popular folk instrument in Assam. It is a stringed instrument made from wood or bamboo.

2 *Gogona* is traditional musical instrument in Assam. It is a jaw harp, a vibrating reed instrument made from bamboo.

men get ready to destroy anyone who threatens another inch of our land.'

The actor nearly topples over from the bamboo pedestal upon which he stood bellowing his speech.

Near hysteria. The applause is deafening. Pradeep smiles. The stage is still for a few seconds before the next scene.

On a cold January morning, Pradeep's father asks him to go to his neighbour Jumon's house and fetch a tool he doesn't have. Jumon's father is out of town, so Jumon has to take care of the cowshed and all the paraphernalia in it. Their respective fathers have always been on friendly, neighbourly terms and often exchange notes on adult matters such as soil type, farm implements, compost and such. Jumon and Pradeep don't share much in common and seldom speak. Pradeep goes to a private, English-medium school and Jumon to a public, Assamese-medium one. Though they did play together as children, their schools separated their lives so much so that now, a polite nod and a hello is the most they exchange on their way to and from school. Pradeep feels a bit annoyed with his father for imposing this errand on him because he does not like interacting much with his own peers, let alone Jumon. Now at least a few courteous sentences would need to be spoken, he is aware, groaning under his breath.

Jumon is arranging the haystack when Pradeep arrives. After a very quick greeting, Jumon asks Pradeep to follow him into the cowshed. He searches for the requested tool as Pradeep waits. *It is taking Jumon unusually long,* Pradeep thinks, *to skim through a very shallow pool of tools and fetch the required one.* He grows impatient. To speed his own exit, he moves forward, stands beside Jumon and bends down to assist in the search. Jumon shifts a bit, their arms nudging slightly against each other. Pradeep suddenly grows conscious of Jumon's breath. He feels something shifting inside him. Jumon finally finds the tool, hands it over to Pradeep and dashes out of the shed, mumbling a quick farewell.

Pradeep returns that very night to return the tool. His father is done with it by dusk but Pradeep waits till after dinner to return it, until something very unfamiliar and uncomfortable settles in his stomach. For some reason, he feels disappointed that Jumon is inside his house and not in the shed. He knocks the main door and Jumon opens. He is alone as his parents are out attending a wedding.

Jumon asks Pradeep if he would like to come to his room. There are some wood carvings he has been working on which he would like to show Pradeep, he says. Pradeep accepts. Once in the room, Jumon shows him the trinkets he has been working on and a few household utilities. They are course and not refined, is what Pradeep thinks, a sense of boredom as well as anxiousness creeping in and making him want to go back home. Just as he is about to state his desire to leave, Jumon turns towards him and cups his scrotum. Not firmly, yet not without intent. Pradeep shudders but does nothing to remove his hand. Instead, he finds his lips moving in an odd synchrony with Jumon's as the unfamiliar and uncomfortable feeling within him bursts open with the help of Jumon's hands.

Over the next three months since, Pradeep and Jumon continue their dance. Mostly in the dark, inside the cowshed, over a pile of hay that Jumon diligently prepares on most days, after their parents and the world around them retreats to a place of stillness. That's when they move.

'FIRE!' Lieutenant Singer commands and a cacophony of firearms take over the stage. The stage lighting is made dramatic with a deep red, signalling the disastrous situation the *raiz mel* attendants find themselves in. The Deputy Commissioner of Nogaon had decided to send Lieutenant Singer and other policemen to break up the swelling peasants' gathering once and for all. When the situation gets tense, Singer takes to violence, probably unaware that it would be the last command of his life. The peasants turn on him, not caring for their own safety, and beat him to death.

The audience watches in silence, except a few wailing infants. Pradeep feels the power of the scene descend like a canopy over the audience and him. The crowd on the stage shouting slogans, trampling their enemy and attacking symbols of foreign tyranny gives Pradeep an adrenaline rush. He feels at one with them. Their angst, their actions are his own; their march to overthrow the oppressors is his own. As he watches, he fights the urge to march onto stage and join the patriots in their defiance. He reminisces about a time in his life when he chose defiance over acceptance. A choice that altered his life forever.

It has been seven days since Jumon was found floating face down in the well by his compound. Nine days since his mother walked in on Jumon and Pradeep naked and entangled on a heap of hay in their den of forbidden love. They were never this careless. Whenever they got a chance to be together, they would stealthily sneak in and out of their den, managing to evade suspicion from both houses by avoiding long, unexplained absences. But nine days ago, they had messed up their own scheme. When Jumon found out that his father would be on his way to the nearby city for work, he felt emboldened. That night, he pinned Pradeep back as he rose to put on his pants.

'Please stay for a bit longer,' he had pleaded.

'You know I can't, Jumon.'

Pradeep now remembers how he gave in without much resistance. He was longing to hear a need in Jumon's voice. A thirst for him. So he stayed. And so he suffers.

It was an ill-fated night for them. Jumon's mother seldom entered the cowshed after dusk. But on that night, she had, to retrieve something inconsequential. She had stood there transfixed, staring blankly at the sight of the two naked boys asleep in each other arms until her son opened his eyes and met hers directly. Everything that happened right after had unfolded in a strange silence. Jumon had leapt to his mother's feet and begun to sob. His mother continued to stand and stare. Pradeep had hastily put on his clothes and rushed out of the scene. Not a word had been uttered.

The two days after the incident had gone by in silence. Pradeep had not left his room until his mother frantically thumped his door screaming his name, compelling him to get out of bed.

'Jumon has killed himself,' she had said.

Pradeep had been present among the other neighbours and even helped retrieve his lover's body from the well. Jumon's mother was silent. Other women began with the customary wails and howls as the corpse was laid on the ground. It was automatic, like turning the light switch on and off—simple. Women mechanically cried for Jumon, who had hardly ever mattered to them. A gap in the usual custom of expressing grief publically was quickly identified and had to be filled, since the mother was not respecting it. Jumon's mother remained silent throughout the commotion. It was construed as shock. A very natural reaction. His father filled in for his wife and cried for both of them.

It has been seven days since then. If words could resuscitate someone, pull back an object from an abyss of guilt, terror and sorrow, Pradeep would latch himself onto every syllable that exists. He would build a ladder with every word he could find to climb his way out of the abyss. But words have failed him. So he resigns to something else, perhaps instinct. Something that just is and that can't be helped.

He goes to his sister's room and sits at her dressing table. She and their parents are getting ready for dinner. He takes out her cosmetic bag and slides a deep shade of scarlet over his lips and ravenous black over his eyelids. He gently pulls down the string of pearls hanging on the corner of the dressing table and puts them over his neck, smiling as he does. His final touch is the stick-on red *bindi* he pulls out of the Sringaar 20-piece pack and places perfectly on the centre of his forehead. Pradeep is himself. No guilt, no fear, as he walks to the table to tell his family that he loved Jumon.

The stage is euphoric; the play at the peak of its narration. Men clad in *dhotis* and armed with sticks, sickles, bows, arrows and whatnot are strewn all over the stage. In a state of mad frenzy, they are attacking everything within their sight, illuminated by an intelligent play of stage lights. A post office, railway tracks, police men. They attack it all. Pradeep thinks that the actors are doing a marvellous job. Their performance is gripping and has a visceral effect on the viewers, the spirit of rebellion escaping their mouths through spit bubbles glistening in the scintillating stage lights Pradeep is close enough to notice.

He knows what to do next. The flickering lights become constant, the loud music recedes and another melancholic tune takes over. The next scene spotlights the faces of a few rioters who are captured by the police. Pradeep takes the cue and moves towards the last props that need to go onstage. He grabs all three of the nooses he had prepared the day before.

They are to be placed in a neat row next to each other, where three prisoners from the mob are to be hanged by the police. This is not the end of the play though. It would end with a dialogue between the Deputy Commissioner of Nogaon and one of his subordinates about how this whole incident had 'shaken' him. How he needs to correspond with his superiors about this 'terribly unfortunate' incident where he was made to look weak. The Crown is no joke, he would say, and the message needs to be imprinted, nay, embossed on the people of this country for all times to come. The playwrights intended to conclude on this note and leave the audience pondering on the significance of this famous peasant rebellion of Assam. Did it indeed shake a giant enemy? Was it episodic enough to ignite the imaginations of the great freedom fighters of Assam a century ago?

Pradeep disapproves of the ending. If it were up to him, he would cut out the last two scenes and end the play with angry peasants hovering over the bodies of dead policemen. The indomitable and unforgettable effect of drama. Alas, he knows that it is not his business. Maybe someday, but definitely not today. For now, he needs to hook the nooses onto the bamboo frame he had constructed with one of the crew members. With the nooses in his hands, he has a fleeting flashback to a time when he had almost made one for himself.

Pradeep has been living in a monastery for almost half a year now. His ribs still hurt from the blows that his father had landed upon him the day he had dressed like a woman, sat on the table and declared his love for the dead Jumon. No questions were asked. His sister sat still and his mother wailed while his father pulled at his hair, slapped him innumerable times, smeared the rouge off of his lips and kicked his balls and ribs and face simultaneously. When Pradeep regained consciousness, he found himself in the same spot on the floor under their dining table. The room was dark; it was dusk. No one seemed to be around. Not even his usual rescuer, his mother. Fueled by the ounce of life he somehow had left in him, he half-crawled to his room and made his way towards one object—his diary. All the while, sharp jabs of pain oozed from his stomach, limbs and crotch, the dried blood on his lips pricking the sides of his mouth. After struggling for a while, he managed to limp out of his house without looking back.

A few thoughts managed to penetrate his throbbing head on his way out. He did not have a penny on him. Nothing except the clothes on his back and his diary. *Where does someone go in such a situation?*

To God.

He found himself making his way to one of the monasteries not very far from his house. It took three hours for his bruised body to carry him to the gates, which would have normally taken no more than half an hour. Once there, he passed out at the front door of the head priest's house. Pradeep only remembers being jolted awake by a rather harsh set hands, with no knowledge of how long he had been unconscious. It was the head priest himself. For the position he held in the minds of devotes, one would anticipate a kind, loving touch from those hands. That clearly wasn't true.

'You would like to live here? As what?' The head priest had asked him.

'A monk.'

'You look too old for that now,' the head priest rebutted, without bothering to ask him where he had suddenly appeared from, why his face resembled a smashed pumpkin or even why he was making such a request. Merely the practicalities of his placement within the monastical establishment were being deliberated, with no further enquiries. Pradeep felt like this was God's work. Who said that the pathway to God would always be soft and kind or strewn with marigolds and fresh, home-made *ghee*? Sometimes it was a pair of rough hands.

In a few moments, the head priest asked him if he could cook, to which he replied in the affirmative. A piece of Pradeep's fate shifted.

Half a year since, and no one from his family has bothered to look for him. Three nights ago, he, too, decided to end his life, like Jumon had. He made a noose by tying together two *gamusas.* Just as he was done making it, there was a knock on the door of the little store room where he lived with potatoes and mice. A young monk had come to inform him that extra food needed to be made for some guests of the head priest. He tossed aside the noose and headed towards the kitchen to do as asked. Later, he got a chance to meet the guests while serving the food. The guests were from a theatre troupe from the nearby town of Barpeta. They had come to spend a few days with the head priest so he could assist them in writing some devotional songs for one of their upcoming plays.

This was God acting for Pradeep yet again. Or so he thought, as he made the most of the brief absence of the head priest and begged them to take him on in their theatre troupe. The guests were taken aback. It was extremely strange to be solicited by a cook from a monastery for a spot in their troupe. They informed him that they were running on full capacity and no longer had any vacancies. God then acted through another set of hands when Pradeep fell on his knees and clutched the hands of one of the guests in desperation, in oblation, begging for any role at all in their theatre company. He finally got offered the spot of a cook, given that this was a new kind of theatre company—a 'mobile theatre', the first of its kind, which would be shifting bases, hopping from place to place and town to town like nomads. Pradeep convinced them that there could never be enough cooks for such an arrangement and that he would work for no payment. He could make do with just a place to stay and leftover food to eat. The set of hands he was holding all along while pleading his case were rough to the touch.

As Pradeep watches the last scene unfold, he can't help but feel a sense of pride, a sense of unshackling and becoming. The sweet taste of breaking out. The courage to defy your fate, perhaps the most important kind of courage one can have and exercise. As he stares at the stage, he smiles to himself at the visuals appearing in his mind.

Little Pradeep in his favourite red shirt and a red pinwheel in his hand, runs unabated in an open meadow. It is just before dusk, although the wind is strong. He is running towards the sun as the pinwheel turns, dizzying him with joy. He crosses a stage, the actors dressed as gods with gold crowns and glass jewels as his family stands next to them, still, unsmiling. There is Jumon, working on a wood-piece sitting atop a pile of hay, naked. Little Pradeep sees it all from the corner of his eyes but the only thing he focuses on is catching the sun before its sets. He runs ahead, the pinwheel fluttering in wild abandon.

Alliances (1986)

In the first month of 1965, on the cold night that Juri had entered the house next door as a new bride, Jamila had watched from across the disfigured bamboo fence between their houses. Jamila's first born, Imtiaz, only a few weeks old at that time, was bundled up like a ball of dough in his mother's arms, wailing like a broken siren. Years later, Jamila would still crack up thinking of Juri's shrill, raucous cries that night, jolting the colony mongrels into a howling chorus as they rallied against the intruding sounds, even more obnoxious than the infant's. Jamila's maternal duties had kept her from fully joining Ujjwal's wedding festivities next door. However, her husband Rashid had not only attended every event but was also a core member of the groom's entourage that had travelled to the nearby Dergaon town to 'collect' the bride. As per custom, the groom's party had to visit the maiden home of the bride where she awaited, adorned in gold, flowers, scents and an intrinsic gloom, for her groom to come and take her away. That night, as Juri entered her new home, another entry was being made in the logbook of woven destinies—the lives of two women whose bonds would permeate into more generations than one.

This is the story of Jameela and Juri.

Rashid, the newcomer Zoology professor from Dibrugarh town, and Ujjwal, the Assamese literature lecturer from Golaghat town, had become quick friends, not just because they were colleagues at Debraj Roy college, but also due to their shared love for local theatre, unsweetened black tea and a disdain for Nehru's handling of India's foreign policy. Rashid's decision to shift to Golaghat town was initially unappreciated by his wife Jameela who insisted on having the support of both their families in raising their newborn son.

Nonetheless, after reading her husband's final offer letter which mentioned his new salary and the additional perks of rent-free accommodation, Jameela swallowed her initial objections and supported the move. For the first few months, Jameela found herself quite insulated in their new albeit small accommodation. Never one to be known for her social skills, Jameela handled her isolation by launching herself headlong into caring for her infant son and husband. She never admitted how much she longed for her family, especially her mother, on whose lap she had rested her head during one too many terrible episodes.

Once Juri moved in next door, a yarn of good neighbourly accord began to form organically between them, transforming steadily into friendship, and eventually gathering into a voluminous web of affection and care. Although it was newer than their husbands' alliance, Jamila and Juri's friendship assumed almost a mystical character. Juri welcomed her son Manas a year after her marriage. This rather simple coincidence of having sons as their firstborn offspring lingered, as the two women conceived again exactly three years later and welcomed their daughters only a few weeks apart.

There were differences, yes. The stark physical contrast between the two women was not lost on people. Jamila's flawless milky skin with a hint of peach and her tall, sturdy frame fuelled the fable around her ancestry that claimed she was of distant Baghdadi stock that had migrated to Upper Assam in the 17th century with the famous Sufi saint and preacher, Ajaan Pir. Her most striking features were the thick, sharply arched eyebrows framing her dark eyes, a testament to their owner's stern persona. Juri, on the other hand, appeared almost inconspicuous next to her friend. A little over five feet, her thin frame looked fragile as her wheatish skin hung loosely over amply protruding bones and very slight muscles. Her broad nose colonised most of her face, although unable to eclipse the spectacle that took place every time she smiled. Two sharply protruding canines illuminated her smile, charming the joyous and the pensive alike. Always the one with solutions to everyone's problems, she was the neighbourhood favourite, whom people entrusted with the responsibility of keeping watch over their children; someone who could be easily asked for a quick hemline stitch.

The differences between the two ran deeper than the shade of their skin. While Jamila's nature was overwhelmingly reserved and she was found unapproachable by most, Juri was the living embodiment of mirth and joviality. When seen together walking to the local market or returning from the Santipur ladies' reading club, clouds of nasty whispers were set afloat by onlookers. Either out of spite due to a lack of such camaraderie in their own lives or plain incomprehension, neighbourhood women would comment 'There go the Memsahab and her Coolie', invoking the image of a moon-skinned British planter's wife sauntering with a dark-skinned native handmaid. Unbeknownst to these gossip mongers and haters were the drops of fate that had begun falling years ago, collecting into a river of mutual respect and pulling the two women into a current of companionship that stood far above their conspicuous differences.

In fact, it was a few days after Juri's wedding, while the two ladies had been sieving rice on their respective verandahs, when Jamila had one of her episodes; an epileptic seizure. Without pausing to consider the lack of prior interaction between them, Juri had dropped her sieve and leapt over the crooked bamboo fence to hold a convulsing Jamila. That day, Juri hadn't merely leapt over the fence; she had dived right into Jamila's heart, in which the most potent reverence for her jumping saviour slowly began to brew. For Jamila, this ailment was an anathema, an abysmal aberration to her unyielding self-control. So when she was vanquished right before a stranger's eyes, her guard dissipated, like that of an enlisted soldier pummeled by an officer before his fellow mates, binding all of them to the silent reception of circumstances, no shame, no pretence. Not one to easily give in to limiting stigmas, Jameela took great care to make slight of this malady and chose to make her presence more visible in public spaces instead, albeit with Juri almost always by her side. For Juri, her generally reticent neighbour's assiduous attempts at ensuring her comfort opened the gateway to a very dependable sisterhood blossoming from the initial neighbourly concern. From swiftly dropping a *gamusa* over a cut bowl of beef upon Juri's arrival, to taking Juri's daughter Moromi to a Sufi baba for miraculous amulets to cure her chicken pox, such acts of thoughtfulness endeared Juri to her next-door neighbour. Over time these acts grew in magnitude, the most recent example being the Hussains clandestinely half-financing Moromi's *tuloni biya,* the symbolic 'first' marriage of a newly menstruating girl in Assamese Hindu tradition to celebrate the commencement of puberty.

Nothing, however, wedged the two women apart as much as their approaches to motherhood. For Jamila, motherhood was God Almighty's way of perpetuating his divine lessons on surrendering to a higher will, of discipline and obeisance. Her two children, Imtiaz and Farnaz, were taught deference to their mother, God, father and teachers, in that order, either through strictures of words or the stick. Never one to betray her emotions to her own children or Juri's, she was of the belief that veneration could be acquired by a love passed on through actions rather than speech or sentimental exhibits. While under her watch, the children of neither house would eat the regular and banal, but only the most flaourful fried *daal*, meat doused in nuts and caramelised onions, and there were always sweets to go with a hearty meal. Yet for the stomachaches, all the children took shelter on Juri's lap, as with the oft-needed hugs when they scraped their knees or their teeth hurt. For more than two decades, this remained the order of things.

Jamila's seasoned impassivity had a brief departure for a few days when her firstborn defied her for the very first time. It was around the time when the mass agitation against the illegal Bangladeshi immigrants was tapering down to its final year, in

1985. Vehemently resolved to make a respectable doctor out of her favourite child, Jamila was livid when he announced his decision to join the Asom Gana Parishad, the political party that had germinated from the seeds of the long and intense agitation that had gripped Assam for six long years.

She was bringing a luscious guava jelly to life on an unseasonably hot October afternoon when Imtiaz had said, 'Amma, I have made up my mind on the issue. I have already informed the college about dropping out and will be leaving for Guwahati next week to start party work.'

The issue was Imtiaz's refusal to get back to a life of 'normalcy' and restart his coursework at the prestigious Dibrugarh Medical College, leaving the dark years of dissent, violence and disruptions behind. Jamila had somehow failed to curb the patriotic fervour from gripping her son as it had the entire state of Assam, carrying its people on a frenzied wave of outcry and protests. She had watched as he used to come home from college during his break and seamlessly join the trend of the time, going on marches, shouting slogans against the foreigners stealing jobs from the likes of his own self. She had watched as Rashid accompanied him on many evenings to Ujjwal's house, whose articles on the menace of the Bangladeshi influx and their presence on the voter's list had acquired tremendous traction among Upper Assam elites. Farnaz sometimes accompanied them.

'I am seventeen! Moromi gets to be there and has already helped Ujjwal *Khura* edit some of his articles. At least I am not out on the streets like Dada,' Farnaz would protest, on being obstructed in her attempts to participate.

Several hours of discussions would ensue between both families on the plight of the *Khilonjia,* the indigenous Assamese. Jamila, who always abstained, was relieved when her children informed her that her husband was just lending his company to those conversations, making himself relevant only with occasional nods and murmurs. Rashid deliberately kept his support tacit, ignoring objections from his best friend and son, for it was not unusual to see fathers burying their children during those times. It was true that the movement was in its sixth year by the time of Imtiaz's patriotic awakening and the young student leaders of the movement appeared more confident about striking a good deal with New Delhi soon. But by not adding any more kindling, Rashid thought he was saving Imtiaz from the fire that ignites within sons on receiving overt support from their fathers. He, too, like Jamila, was hoping that this 'phase' in his son's life would pass and that he would return to his journey towards becoming the first doctor in his entire bloodline. So the day Imtiaz announced his resolve to leave his coveted seat at the medical college, Jamila's stoic exterior cracked like the earth's crust after violent tectonic activity.

'You immature fool!' she had shouted at Imtiaz, waving her sticky ladle violently in the air as she spoke. 'Is it not enough that you made it out alive from that inferno? And don't you forget for a second that the tide can turn against your circumcised dick anytime, like those sleeping peasants at Nellie, butchered like the goat I stew for you lot!'

Imtiaz had been rattled, not just by what he considered an untimely explosion from a dormant volcano, but by the narrowness of his mother's assumptions about their honourable movement.

'How can you make the issue so petty, Amma?' he countered. 'Do you think it's about religion? And since when have you become so conscious about this? Half the time you are donating money to this or that temple with Juri *Khuri*. Frankly, I am ashamed that you, my mother, would belittle the movement this way. Never mind...why bother with you, when have you ever budged from your throne of thoughts anyway!'

Imtiaz had started to walk away when the ladle came flying towards him, slapping him on his left shoulder, leaving a sticky goo of pinkish-lavender jelly where it struck.

'Have you gone mad?!' he had blurted out, jerking from the force of the blow. As he faced his attacker with indignation, he saw her arching her eyebrows to reach their highest summit, the pupils below sparkling with heat. She then spoke very slowly, as if by design, to ensure that each word would sink into the very being of her mutinous son.

'Your father has worked very hard to put you through medical school and here you are, throwing it away like an entitled brat. You told us you were too young to understand the movement when it started and now that you had matured, you want to be more involved. We agreed. What you did before was fine, all that placard carrying and fist pumping during your recess from medical school. And I am sure it was your voice that carried all the way to New Delhi and led to the accord being signed. But this…this dangerously stupid turn you've taken won't be accepted. You think Manas would ever do something like this to his parents? He is only a year younger than you. He could have chosen to do as you did but he knew better and stuck with his books. Says he is preparing for the civil service exams, and wants to become a public servant to be of true service to his people. Juri is so proud. Do you think gallivanting around town like a *goonda* pleading for votes is how you serve your people?'

'Who exactly are you calling a *goonda,* Amma?' Imtiaz snapped at this, cutting his mother's cold narration short, the mercury rising in his blood. 'Those who are bold enough to speak for the true people of our land? As for your darling Manas, he is a bloody coward! Ujjwal *Khura* knows it too. An excuse for a true son of the soil. What good will he do as a high-class officer? Some good old boot-licking for mainlanders whose only vision for Assam is her perennial subjugation?'

Jamila had had enough. Her pride pierced, every last ounce of patience lost, she spoke to her son with a tone of finality.

'Go then. And never show me your face again.'

'Jamila *baiti*, let's make the next batch with sweetened coconut instead of sesame. I think two dozen of each kind will be enough for the *pithas* to start with. Rest can be done on the spot if needed.' Juri advised her friend, who she noted was more sombre than usual.

She was certain that Jamila's gloom on this festive occasion of Magh Bihu was on account of Imtiaz. It had been a year since his departure for Guwahati. As the families learnt later, things were far from amicable between the two when he left. Jamila being Jamila had resolved to emerge unscathed from her misery, at least in the eyes of those watching, gossiping, pitying. Just a week after Imtiaz's departure, Jamila set about her daily life as though nothing had happened, even as it took months for Rashid to come to terms with it. Only Farnaz wrote to him regularly, strictly abiding by her brother's insistence to neither show nor discuss the contents of his responses with either of his parents. Not that Jamila cared; for her, Farnaz was her only child. And Rashid knew better than to irk Jamila by visibly concerning himself with news of a son who had defied them. Defied *her*. Despite these hostilities, Juri was sure that it had taken her friend every ounce of her strength to retain her composure this time, far more than what was required to overcome the violent convulsions that occasionally took possession of her body.

'Hmmm, you are right. This way, there will be a variance in the *pithas*, much better than having just one kind. I will quickly finish the next batch and start with the *laddoos*.' Jamila pondered over her friend's advice while carefully folding the sides of the rice pancake with a spatula and her forefinger to cover the sweet black sesame stuffing at the center, pressing it down in the heated pan for just enough time to shape it into the much-loved delicacies.

For nearly two decades, the two families had celebrated Magh Bihu together. Ever since this tradition took root, every year, the Hussains would gather in the compound of the Boras on Uruka, the night of feasts, before the morning of Magh Bihu. The scope of work and division of labour for the feast would be set beforehand. The young scions would collect the firewood, bamboo and other materials and set about constructing the *meji*, the hay and wood structure to be ceremonially burnt as a mark of respect to the fire gods the morning after. A welcome change of duty transferred to the children by Rashid and Ujjwal as they grew up. The duo could then naturally find more time to devote due diligence to their task of collecting the raw materials for all the delectable items that would be cooked to perfection by their wives. Pounded rice for the *pithas*, dry coconut, puffed rice, jaggery, black and white sesame for *laddoos*, yam, *patha* mutton and *sitol* fish for the main course. The ladies would begin to cook the light snacks before dusk, and as the customary bonfire of bonhomie emerged by nightfall, all members of both households took turns in cutting, washing, mixing, and stirring what cooked above the *souka,* a clay stove that added an extra smoky flavour to everything on its flame.

This would be their first Magh Bihu without Imtiaz. One vacant spot around the bonfire. The human transistor box—as Farnaz and Moromi had titled him for his booming voice which used to serenade them with the most moving Bhupen Hazarika songs—would be amiss. The most clandestine corner of Jamila's mind sprouted these thoughts which she then managed to pluck away. But not before she let the smoke from the *souka* flood her eyes with warm tears.

'The cold is bone-chilling today,' Rashid told Ujjwal as he rubbed his hands frantically to produce extra heat despite his close proximity to the crackling bonfire.

'*Xosa*,[1] the fog is also so dense; I wonder where Manas and Farnaz are,' said Ujjwal, more as a question than a response to Rashid's statement.

The bonfire was already ablaze. Rashid and Ujjwal were butchering the mutton into smaller pieces with a small *dao*, keeping one hand free for the yam chips their wives were frying for everyone to munch on.

'Have you seen those two?' Ujjwal asked Moromi, who was peeling onions seated on a low tool besides her mother and Jamila.

At this, Moromi briskly got up from her place, mumbling something about the onions destroying her eyes, and trotted back to the house to splash them with cold water.

Juri, intent on chopping the yams as finely as possible for Jamila to fry, spoke without looking up, 'Maybe they have gone to say hello to their friends near the mission school. Farnaz was yapping the other day about a big *meji* construction at one of her friends' places, about ten feet high, something to do with a new beginning after the horrible years that have gone by. Said this Bihu is particularly special, truly a new year to look forward to, so one couldn't possibly make do with a normal looking *meji*.'

She suddenly caught her breath as the last words left her lips. She should have known better than to allude to

1 'True' in Assamese

anything that could remind Jamila about the *andolan*, about Imtiaz.

Thankfully, Jamila continued the thread of the conversation by asking whether Manas would manage to cycle the two of them back home, given how dense the fog was.

It was past eleven. The aura in Ujjwal's compound had changed by then to one of anxiety and anger. Manas and Farnaz were still missing. The food was half cooked, courtesy their preoccupied minds. Ujjwal and Rashid had set out looking for them, mounted on their bicycles, one hand on the handle and the other clutching battery-run torches to pierce the opaque night. Enroute Mission Road, they asked several people, neighbours and acquaintances alike, if they had spotted the two youngsters that evening or night, together or alone. There wasn't much to describe what Manas looked like. Given his regular features, average height and unremarkable complexion, an enquiry on such lines could hardly be of use for the search party. The same couldn't be said for Farnaz, who shared similar physical distinctions with her mother. Shorter than Jamila by an inch, with her 5'6' frame, she was still taller than most her high-school friends. If her mother's complexion could be described as a blend of milk and peaches, hers was milk with a drop of vermillion, adding a rosy tint to her skin that deepened around her cheeks, made more pronounced with her high cheekbones. Her thick jet-black hair dangled way below her waist, and hardly an eye could avert itself when her long braid swung as she walked to school. So after a few failed attempts, when Rashid saw the *muezzin* of the mosque on Mission Road, who was a renowned exorcist, he asked him right away if he had seen his tall, fair daughter. The *muezzin* replied, 'Yes, on the road towards Santipur, holding hands with a boy.'

Juri was sobbing uncontrollably, covering her mouth with a fistful of her *sador*[2] to keep herself from wailing aloud. Moromi pranced around the compound nervously. Jamila sat by the fire, solemnly staring at the disintegrating logs without blinking.

'Lord O Lord, please protect our children,' Juri kept mumbling in between her cries, eyes squeezed in concentration as though open eyes could disrupt the transmission of a prayer.

'Do not assume the worst, Juri, let the men come back first. They have only been gone a few minutes,' Jamila reassured Juri, not looking at her, staring at the fire.

2 The term *sador* comes from *mekhela sador,* the traditional two-piece attire of Assam. The *mekhela* is the bottom portion, a type of cylindrical skirt and the *sador* is the drape that goes around the upper body.

Just as these words were spoken, an apparition started taking form across the rickety iron gate on the other side of the bonfire. Jamila was the first one to notice and as the lock on the iron gate clanked open, she stood up.

Moromi shrieked, 'Dada!'

Juri opened her tightly squeezed eyes at the sound of Moromi's voice, running towards the gate through which Manas and Farnaz had just walked in, hand in hand. On seeing the two together, fingers interlocked, Juri stopped a few paces before them, staring at their joint hands in confusion. The world fell silent for all the parties standing within the Bora compound for a few moments.

After what felt like an entire earthly revolution around the sun, Jamila spoke up, sternly. 'What's this?' she asked, casting a scathing look at her daughter.

Farnaz had her eyes fixed on the ground.

'Jamila *borma*,[3] I want to explain,' started Manas but Jamila held up her palm, making him halt midway.

'I am speaking to my daughter. Let her answer,' she continued, without taking her eyes off Farnaz.

At this, Farnaz drew in a breath like the cows she had seen pinned to the ground, a few seconds before meeting their fate on Bakr-Id. Looking up to face her mother, she blurted a string of words without a break.

---

3 *Borma* refers to one's mother's older sister in Assamese

'We love each other and I know you and Abba would never approve. I asked him to elope with me tonight and get married. It is not his fault. Because he wouldn't hear a thing about us eloping, I left a letter in his room today to meet me at the bus depot at nine to catch the last bus to Dimapur. He came, but he refused to go with me and convinced me to come back home for everyone's approval of our relationship. I swear...' Her desperate monologue was interrupted with a sharp slap across her face. Jamila's hand outpaced Manas's protective reflexes and as Farnaz foundered into her lover's arms, Juri sped to the spot where the pair stood, as if suddenly having thawed from a frozen state. '*Baiti*,[4] wait!' she yelped, casting a pitiful glance at Farnaz. Then gripping her son's shoulders, she started shaking him as she asked, 'Why didn't you ever say something to us?'

Jamila turned now to look at her best friend, as if seeing her for the very first time and said, 'What do you mean by why he didn't say anything? What's there to say if all was already done? His scheming mind had already taken hold of my young girl when he should have been a brother figure to her!'

On this unanticipated attack, Juri turned away from her son and politely said, '*Baiti*, what scheming are you talking about? Farnaz said they are in love. It takes two for that.'

'Love!' Jamila scoffed. 'How are you calling this love, Juri? How do you think a seventeen-year-old girl can decide to set

4 *Baiti* refers to one's elder sister in Assamese

off on the path of love? Someone has to show the way. In fact, hold on, let me get all the facts clear first.' She turned towards Moromi, who was quietly lurking under the tall coconut tree a few feet away, shielding herself from the arrows of accusations. She was dragged to the spotlight when Jamila shouted, 'Moromi! Come here this instant.' Always fearful of her aunt Jamila, she scuffled her feet towards where everyone stood and looked at the ground.

'Did you know about this? This, what you call it…affair?' Jamila shot the question right at Moromi, who was as silent as a stone. 'Moromi! I am asking you again, answer me! NOW!'

The rise in Jamila's pitch shook her bones as she whispered, 'Ye…yes, I knew…I…I mean I found out only a month ago.'

'A month ago!' Jamila thundered. 'How long has this been transpiring? And how have the three of you dirty-minded, shameless urchins managed to conceal this? Moromi, do you study at all in school or just pass filthy love notes from your brother to Farnaz?'

'*Baiti*…please…listen!' Juri interjected, her sentiments battered, the acid thrown on Moromi sizzling her flesh instead.

'*Baiti*,' she continued, 'why blame Moromi? This is a shock, but do we need to point fingers at anyone? Aren't they all our children? Have we not raised them together? Is Farnaz any less of a daughter to me than Moromi is to you? Let's first thank God Almighty that the children are safe and back home, and then sit down to discuss this matter.' Juri finished on this hopeful note of having doused a bit of the fire, even though her own head was still swirling at the bizarre turn of her Uruka night.

'Oh, discuss the matter! Discuss, she says! Discuss what exactly, Juri? How your good-for-nothing son seduced my young daughter? Discuss how you and your family encouraged this? After all, where will your goof of a son ever find someone like Farnaz? Discuss what now…wedding arrangements for a child bride? Have you an inkling of the scandal all of this will cause if word gets out?' Jamila rumbled, now pointing her finger straight at Juri.

Her mouth now completely dry after all the vile words that had shot out of her best friend's mouth, Juri felt something snap inside her.

'*Bas*, *Baiti*, enough,' Juri retaliated, feeling her face heat up. 'You call my son a goof, a schemer, a seducer, but see no role of your daughter in all of this? What about all those nights she came over to my house with Imtiaz and Rashid *da* to discuss the *andolan*? Now that I recall, she insisted on taking tea to Manas's room every single night she was there, when he would be busy studying. Quite a freedom fighter she turned out to be, didn't she?'

'Ma, please…' managed Manas, touching his mother's arm softly, extremely taken aback by this unfamiliar persona taking over his otherwise composed mother.

'So you let it happen, then. I am right. You didn't stop this abomination. I am really beginning to wonder what is behind this scheme of yours.' Jamila jumped right in with these words, adding more layers to the pile of blame she was throwing at Juri.

'What "scheme" do you keep blabbering about?' Juri spat out with disgust in her voice. 'The children have all grown up together for years. How was I to know anything odd could be happening?' She finished with a question while turning towards her house, meaning to walk into it and rest her spinning head on her pillow.

She had taken less than six steps when an exaggerated, vitriolic laughter stopped her on her path. Jamila had taken a seat by the fire and was letting out spurts of laughter, closing her eyes, slapping her knees and shaking her head as if to throw off the funny notions swimming in her mind.

As if compelled by an external force, Juri found herself involuntarily asking, 'What are you laughing about?'

'Me?' Jamila quipped mockingly. With wide wandering eyes accompanied by an elusive smile, she continued, 'As I see it, Juri, your son turned out to be as much an *andolankari* as mine, although in a different way. Mine left to save the *Khilonjia*, yours risks it all to make one out of my daughter by smearing her head red with vermillion. I see why you or Ujjwal would even consider entertaining this. At least he came of *some* use.'

There was no more laughter as Juri and Jamila now faced one another after this speech. They looked right into each other's eyes—one seated, one upright; two cocks inside a fighting ring sizing each other up.

It was Juri who made the first move, 'I have been hearing this for many years now, that you are a difficult person. And I have seen you be that way too. Especially with your son. But I never allowed myself to think that you might be completely mad as well. You have proved it tonight. *You are mad.* And our sons are not the same,' she continued her tirade, 'Mine will never abandon me. And we are not the same. I will never drive my children out of my life.'

Her last sentence was the dart that hit the bullseye, and the bull leapt into action.

For all the witnesses present, what happened next would remain at once a blur, a flash of lighting, and a suspension of time for posterity. A pouncing Jamila grabbing Juri's hair, a clawing Juri clutching Jamila's blouse, ripping off the right sleeve. The men who had just arrived from their failed search attempt dropping their cycles and plunging into the duel, trying to separate the entangled women. A frightened Moromi, sobbing, standing next to the bonfire that illuminated the scene like the theatre her father loved to watch with her Rashid *Bordeuta*. Manas shifting from one foot to the other, not knowing how to join the fire-fighting squad. Farnaz staring at the sight before her, the corner of her eye mindful of the few people peering into their compound. The battle abruptly ending with Jamila's body contorting in her husband's grip, mistaken at first for attempts to break free. When her body went rigid and her eyes travelled back into her skull, primary witnesses recalled Juri manoeuvring away from Ujjwal's hands, running to the collapsing figure, pulling it away from near the bonfire, cradling the head in her lap, screaming for water.

Years later, when Manas and Farnaz's teenage son Adam teased his grandmother, Jamila *Nani*, about looking 'gangster' with the thick-rimmed black glasses given to her after cataract surgery, his Juri *Aita-ma* rocking beside her in a chair smirked, 'This oldie is a gang leader. Ask her about the Uruka Night of 1986.'

Colour My Grave Purple (1980-2000s)

As strange as it sounds, Sara believed in mystical signs. With more dedication than anyone else she knew, she looked for signals and cues to make sense of puzzling incidents or sentiments. For instance, why did she inevitably end up sharing the closest bonds with Scorpio sun signs? Their obvious arrogance and underlying serial killer instincts were common knowledge. But despite all her resistance, Scorpios kept stinging their way into her life. Perhaps she was being rewarded by the universe for some reason, with an abundant supply of a very valuable trait that defined Scorpios—loyalty. Of course, there were exceptions to the rule, like everything in the universe.

She would often make deductions and draw celestial connections to make sense of many things that happened around her. It helped her process and eventually accept events that didn't make sense when they first occurred. Like how despite having top grades and a good co-curricular certificate from her previous school, she could not get into the school of her choice for the two years of pre-university; one which many of her old school friends were getting into. Her parents did not enquire about what went wrong. They were happy that she was left with no option but to join a school of *their* choice. She hated them for their victory.

'This school is strict about academics and that's what matters,' her father had said when she had protested.

After she finished her board exams, her usually easygoing father became suddenly serious about her studies; rather uncharacteristic behaviour for him. Her parents were never overwhelmingly strict about things like grades, unlike many of her friends' parents. Maybe they were scared of seeing a repeat of what had happened with their elder son Ziyad, who had suddenly stopped speaking when he was in the 8th grade. Perfectly healthy and 'normal' up until he was fourteen, he then began to withdraw from everyone, starting with his own parents, and only spoke to himself or his 'own people' whom no one could see but him. He was five years older to Sara.

'Childhood schizophrenia,' the doctors had declared, asking Abba and Amma if they had put too much pressure on him to study or if he had suffered significant trauma in his early childhood. Abba and Amma had no answers. And therein, Sara deduced, lay the reason behind their extra cautious behaviour with her. Not that it bothered her much. She didn't really mind studying and her grades were above average. She just didn't think it necessary to have the first twenty elements of the periodic table memorised in serial order. For Sara, apart from the occasional reprimand, 'You should focus more in class, Sara. We are tired of your teachers complaining about your wavering attention', there were never any serious consequences to her B plus dipping to a C minus in physics. It just meant more home tuitions during the vacations.

It hardly took any time for her to realise why she found herself at her current school. She was meant, nay, *destined* to find herself in a place she hadn't chosen, because she was being re-directed towards love. Her first 'real' love, a relationship. She was sixteen, and was beginning to worry about herself when no crush would translate into something more, as it did for her friends who were already in long-term relationships which had crossed the one-year mark.

Her time had finally arrived. She found Rohit Hazarika. The cute basketball player from the Science stream, one year her senior, who bunked his practical classes and waited by the water dispenser to meet her. He would cross the corridor by her classroom very slowly, hoping she would get the hint. And she did. She would excuse herself to go to the bathroom and turn towards the corner where the water dispenser stood, a grinning Rohit standing next to it. He would give her a chocolate bar (so she could like him more), or a cassette of his favourite rock band, like Poison or Guns and Roses (so she could get to know him more). She loved getting to like him more and know him more. She was content.

Two months later, her father died. As a police officer, he was posted in a remote part of Assam, and on the weekend of his passing, he was visiting his family in Guwahati. His job was such that he kept getting transferred from one end of Assam to another every two to three years, sometimes sooner. His last posting was in a place very far from Guwahati city, where she now permanently stayed along with her mother and brother on account of her schooling.

That weekend was the one after Sara's 16th birthday, which Abba had missed. She was upset, but she knew he would make up for it. *That* night during *that* weekend, Sara was jolted awake by her mother who had whispered to her, 'Abba is in the hospital.' She asked why.

Heart attack, her mother calmly explained. Oddly, the first thought that popped up in her mind (like the gopher on her favourite mobile game) was the date. It was 11th September when they had gone to bed. The falling twin towers had been repeating on their television screen while they were having dinner, a reminder of what had gone wrong in the world. She looked at the round clock with the Roman numbers on the wall opposite her. It was easy to read; the lights were on. It was

2 am. 12 September 2004; a date marking her Abba slipping into an oblivion from where he could never be retrieved, no matter the amount of love, longing or prayer.

She visited him once in the two days he was kept alive on life support at the Intensive Care Unit. She softly touched the only part of him that his stingy tubes allowed her to, the palm of his right hand. It was cold and unfamiliar. When she came home that day, her mind set itself to work, searching for any signs that this was written in her fate. When he passed away two days later, it was crystal clear to her. Why would he suddenly happen to visit Guwahati that very weekend? He was *meant* to be with his family when he passed. What about the sudden emphasis on her grades and studies in general? Wasn't this a signal that she would soon have to pull up her socks, do well, get through a good college, get a good job, become responsible, and take care of her family? Why, before going to bed that night, had he suddenly summoned her to sit beside him and give her a sermon on why family is the most important thing in the world, the only thing that is real, that matters?

'Friends will come and go but your family shall always remain. Always take care of your family and never do anything to upset them,' Abba had said.

Why? Certainly, he must have had a premonition that he would not be around for long? It couldn't be mere coincidence.

The universe was signalling to her that her world was going to turn upside down. Irrevocably. Forever.

It was Abbas' first death anniversary. Her relatives had come from different parts of Assam to be with her family and commemorate the deceased. Her mother had organised a reading of the Quran by the *Ulema* to be followed by a *dua*, a prayer for the departed. Sara loathed the sounds that floated into her room, penetrating her closed door as though defying her. She was howling, barely able to breathe. She hated the sounds of a faith that kept her away from her Abba. She was not allowed to visit his grave earlier that morning when an all-male group including her brother, who was much more functional and 'normal' now, had gone to pay their respects and pray beside his grave at a cemetery in the heart of Guwahati. She had gone there only once before, the day after he was buried. She had stood outside the iron gate and looked inside and was shocked to find how reduced her Abba's final home was. A six by four mound on earth?

'You are lucky that his grave is just by the gate, so you can see it without entering,' an uncle had whispered in her ears. She wanted to hit him.

The morning of the first death anniversary, Sara had a huge fight with Amma, who mostly listened to Sara yell at her.

The uncles who were present had told her she couldn't go with them to the cemetery.

'She is a woman. The *Shariat* forbids it,' they said.

Amma had remained silent and Sara had locked herself in her room since then. Before her self- imposed isolation, she stopped by Abba's study and picked up the huge stack of his personal journals. Her father, the journal addict. He'd written so many of them over so many years. He was often seen scribbling something under the light of a lamp, another one of his favourite objects. No matter the location of his posting or the conditions of the quarters he was assigned, a lamp would always be fixed at his bedside or study table. Sometimes there were long gaps. It was natural. But he would always remember to resume his writing. No one from the family had picked up this habit. Once their own permanent home was built, Abba found a special place for his precious journals.

'People would never guess that a chair can hold so many secrets,' he had said, his eyes twinkling as he pulled open a compartment built into the underside of his wooden office chair. It was the ingenious creativity only her father was capable of. Amma had rolled her eyes and Sara had giggled; she loved Abba's funny antics and quirks. It was rather disappointing when after his death, the only other secrets the box spilled apart from his journals were the property and bank loan papers for the construction of their house.

When Sara heard the synchronised prayers from her room, she clutched a few of the journals, drawing them close to her chest; tears and snot dripping on them. She was asking Abba for a sign. Something, *anything,* that could assure her that all of this would go away. That her pain would go away. Rohit had gone off to college, leaving Assam, and was not there for her the way she would have liked. And though she met her friends every day at school and often spoke on the phone afterwards, they couldn't *really* understand. She couldn't talk to Amma. She obviously couldn't talk about Rohit to Amma, lest she disowned her.

That's when she decided to take matters into her own hands, to look for the signs herself. She made a plan to pick out random pages from Abba's journals over the next few days and see whether there was anything special in there. One page a day. She wanted to find the words of wisdom she was sure she would mystically bump into inside her father's journals. She would seek out her own solace; she didn't need anyone.

28th September 1983, North Cachar Hills

Received a letter today from my university friend Indra. I got terribly excited, since it's not easy for a letter to find its way to Sontilla, so secluded in the hills. The first correspondence outside of my family in a long time. Made me feel lonelier than I should allow myself to feel. The agitation against the foreigners is peaking, he writes. I knew that, of course, but perhaps he thinks my remote posting in these hills has made me less aware. Last I heard, his brothers were active members of the student's union at the forefront of the agitation to drive the illegal Bangladeshis out of Assam. The two are often seen leading marches in our hometown. He has only written one sentence about this; the rest is all about his newborn son. I respect that he understands my position. Sometimes I think it's for the best that I am isolated here. Slims my chances of getting law and order duty against the agitators. I am sure to bump into several of my own friends in those crowds. Imagine having to baton your own buddies? How would I distinguish myself from them then? Only through my uniform, the natural divide… I am missing Ziyad terribly today. I keep tracing the shape of his tiny face, the button nose, the little pink lip which opened liked a fish's mouth when I touched it with honey on my fingertip. He is three months and twenty-five days old today. Still can't believe Naziya and I are parents now…

Sara closed the journal, flabbergasted that the very first page she had read was an entry from September, the month that Abba left her. Definitely a sign. Lesson learnt for the day—gear up for horrible Septembers for the rest of your life.

5th July 1985, Nalbari

Finally reached home a few hours ago. It's nearly midnight but I feel like I have to write something to fall asleep. Spent the day in office, business as usual. Just before I left, was informed about a girl found 'dead under mysterious circumstances.' In one of the immigrant villages. Went to the inquest right away. The body was kept on the ground, a circle of people hovering around, trying not to disturb her father who was squatting beside it, his eyes downcast. Mother was beating her chest and head, bawling and scratching her own face. The girl was hardly eleven or twelve. Later confirmed she was twelve. A big blood stain and spots on her frock. Visible signs of strangulation on her neck. Two objects were retrieved from her private area. A candle and a blade. The blade was rusted. The girl had gone missing yesterday night when she had ventured out to go to the toilet. Her body was found today morning, dumped in a ditch. No matter how many horrors I see as a police officer, I never seem to be prepared for the next. I am still surprised. And that surprises me. I feel sick. Every time. Dead body sent for post-mortem but no points for guessing what happened to her. I couldn't help but notice the body was kept below an Ezar tree, the Queen's crepe-myrtle. Dense with bright, purple blossoms. How beautifully the branches fell towards the ground, as if beckoning to her to come and join them in her spirit abode. As though the branches were aware of the order of things. The site was ghastly and poetic. The inquiry is on. We have a few suspects already. The drill starts tomorrow. I pray for her and hope when I close my eyes tonight, I don't see those blood stains on her frock...

19 March 1986, Nalbari

My bee-hive box is finally done. I am really excited to start my apiculture journey. I promised myself to find time for it. Sometimes I wonder what my life would have been like in the village, like my father wanted it to be. A few days before he passed, completely bedridden, he even confessed why he would often beat me when he found me with a book in my hand—so that I wouldn't study further and leave them behind. Who would take care of the rice fields, it seems! So strange that it is the other way round for so many people I know. Almost all the people I know. Maybe bee-keeping will be the closest I will ever be to a life of that sort. He said he was proud of me just hours before he passed. That deep down he always harboured a desire to see me in uniform as he had once hoped for himself. But the idea seemed farther away than the stars so to waste time on it felt criminal. I remember being shocked. I held his hand and cried so much that the bed shook. It may seem like I am making this up but I swear he used this metaphor. My father, who never spoke more than two sentences at a time to me. As if he knew he was going to go soon and that he had to make right something that was tenuous between the two of us. I had gone back home during a break from the police training academy. Four years gone already. I am sure wherever he is right now, my father knows that the motive is definitely not to feel close to my roots. I just find the mechanical organisation of bees captivating.

Sara couldn't read on. Her eyes were flooded with fresh, hot tears. She felt so close to him in that moment. Just like her, he, too, extracted mystical signals from his surroundings. He too perceived some kind of premonition in his father's last words, in retrospect. Just as she had, in his. In retrospect. To Sara, this was a major sign that she had to honour his last words to her. No matter how much it hurt to see Amma only pray all the time instead of talking to her, she had to find a spot of amicability. Be the cement that kept her grieving family together.

23 December 1990, Silchar

'Say hello to your Type 2 diabetic friend! Got the results today. Naziya is nervous. Maybe it's not too bad. I will check my diet and exercise more. Just wasn't expecting it at this age. My mother doesn't have it and my father got it much later, in his late sixties. I trust Naziya, though, in her capacity for care. On another note, I managed to get a few Ezar saplings. I have put myself on a mission. I will plant Ezar trees in all my accommodations, wherever I am posted. It takes around a decade for the tree to mature and knowing I won't witness flowers of my own doing

will pinch a little. But! Imagine those in whose tenures they will. And how they will sing praises for the man who thought up this sensitive scheme. The world needs to be flooded with such beauty.

23 February 1994, Tinsukia

Today I envy those who can drown in drink and calm their nerves. The bodies of the five men were brought into the police station today. Bullet-ridden bodies, one's eyes gouged out, tongues sliced, nails removed, knee caps shattered. Bodies bore other marks of severe torture.

The spiral begins. In fact, it has already begun.

Newspapers report death by army encounter of five ULFA militants. Public screaming fake encounter, extra-judicial killing. Court orders flouted when the nine men picked up by the Indian Army were asked to be presented before a magistrate. Four of them were released. Not by the Magistrate, of course, but by the Army. In the middle of the night, in a forest. They were asked to run for their lives. The trigger wasn't pulled behind them as they obeyed the command and fled towards their own freedom.

As for the other five, their foul-smelling corpses made an appearance at the police station. The Army is convinced that they were ULFA militants, trying to set up camp in a forest. Their families and even the other lucky four who were released claim otherwise. That the tortured and slain were only petty traders. The mess is easy to see. It is almost a pattern in the state now. Our word against theirs. People's word against the Army's and vice versa.

A week earlier, five masked men, suspected ULFA militants, shot and murdered the manager of a tea estate. Couldn't pay the ULFA's extortion demand as was reported. The names of the nine men were hand-picked by the Army from the entry log of the estate. One, a student leader, dead. Another, the brother of an ULFA cadre, released. One of the colonels is apparently related to the murdered manager. The labyrinth deepens. Police played like pawns. Anger rises among the people. What is the proof? Show us! People are shouting, whilst the ULFA prowls within and outside the ranks of system, lengthening this labyrinth we deserve to get out of. I don't even think it is safe to write of it. I will sign off.

8 May 1997, Karbi Anglong

I am at a loss with Ziyad. I am not seeing any progress with his situation. He has lost so much weight. When I tried to hold his hand today, he leapt out of the seat, as if it had caught on fire. He began screaming. Not at me but something else. He ran around the room, holding his ears, squeezing his eyes shut until two orderlies had to grab him and hold him down until he got calmer. Naziya hardly speaks much and spends hours in her room sleeping. Sara shouldn't have to see all this. I have decided to get my leave sanctioned anyhow and take him to Bangalore for a better consultation...

15 October 1997, Karbi Anglong

Sixteen militants surrendered before me today from the 8th battalion of the ULFA. There was a woman among them. A petite girl, no more than twenty, although her face bore the burden of age. It was evident she was with child. Her eyes were lowered throughout and she was hardly audible in her replies to the questions we asked her. I could tell that she was making efforts to not break down. It did not last long. Before being sent off to the transit camp, she burst into tears and kept asking us to bring back her infant. I could gather between her sobs that she had left her very young child behind. I asked where the father was, searching for a face to come up from among the surrenderers. When no one did, I gathered through her incoherent words that he was already 'martyred', as she put it. I did not press further and told her we would try to find her child.

13 April 1998, Guwahati

We watched a Hollywood film called Titanic today at Apsara Cinema Hall. I can avow it is the most marvellous thing I have seen on screen. How have we humans managed to get this far, I wonder. To be able to capture and translate a tragedy of that magnitude and difficulty into controlled storytelling. Did they actually shoot in the sea? Escapes me. Was skeptical about taking Zaid but with God's grace he was calm throughout and seemed to have enjoyed the popcorn. I was mortified when the nude scenes suddenly popped up so unexpectedly. I tried to check Sara's face with the corner of my eyes. Her mouth was open. Shit. Naziya froze beside me, I could tell. Many started whistling and clapping in the hall and in that moment, I thanked the heavens for my privilege of being able to watch from the box. Awkward silence when we got into our car later so I tried a diversion tactic and started a poll for the two movies that have released simultaneously. Titanic and Duplicate, the latter with the King of Bollywood and Sara's heartthrob, Shah Rukh Khan. Sara's allegiance has shifted and she had firmly declared that she will only ever marry the blonde actor from Titanic.

30 May 1999, Guwahati

We dropped our little Sara at the boarding school today. I don't think I have enough words to describe my feelings at the moment. It was as if I left behind a pound of flesh from my own heart when I said bye to her from the gates of her hostel. Had it not been for Naziya pressing my arm every now and then, I swear I would have started crying. Sara was solemn and calm and managed her best smile while waving us goodbye. I know her better than that, she must have been broken inside. I know my baby. I wonder what she is doing right now. As per school rules, we will get to speak over telephone only once a month but can write to each other regularly. How I will get through this, I have no idea. We had no choice but to do this. It wasn't healthy for her to be witnessing Ziad's deterioration…

5 July 2001, Tezpur

I went to attend the wedding of one of my security guards today, a little on the outskirts of the town. I can't help but write about the experience of being taken back to my childhood days, when weddings were a hub of erratic activities and not the organised orchestrations we witness nowadays in towns and cities. The family made special arrangements for my comfort (or so they thought), isolating me from the general crowd of guests, reserving their drawing room for me to sit in, with additional stand fans brought in for cooling, a lavish spread of all kinds of dry fruits, sweets, juices and tea for their most coveted guest. Oh, their faces when I insisted on sitting with the rest of the guests and then ate with them on areca palm plates, my hands digging deep into the sour fish curry. It was a day wedding and I was sweating like a pig but who cares! People sat on rickety wooden benches while servers came in carrying rice in buckets and served it with mugs. A departure from my village days where we sat on the ground in open fields, at times only half-sheltered by shamianas erected mainly to keep the cows away, instead of aesthetic considerations. I loved the experience. The dessert was another classic from childhood, fresh curd with rasgullas. On my way back, I noticed that the Ezar trees were in full bloom, adorning both sides of the road, my car moving under a canopy of pink and purple jewels of nature. It was breathtaking. I don't even remember when exactly I fell asleep, like I was lulled by the sight. I woke only when I arrived back at the bungalow and felt as if I had been asleep for a century. I have been feeling fresh since, and before I sign off today, I want to commit to myself that the procrastination ends tomorrow. I will begin the novel. The plot is finally as clear as morning dew in my mind.

24 November 2001, Tezpur

I wonder if we are ever truly aware of how the name of our home gets synonymously used with violence and insurgency. It's an automatic identification by those beyond the chicken neck. The mainstream media (whenever they are gracious enough to find us 'newsworthy') does its fair share of damage. Are we even disturbed by it? Or are we so entangled in the maze of our sufferings of the past two decades that this narrative has become part of us? Do we want to change it?

I was at a dinner party at Sara's school today for Foundation Day when I joined a group of men chatting animatedly. They were mostly tea garden managers and businessmen. We introduced ourselves to each other and found that some of our kids went to the same class. We got to talking and one of the persons who had recently joined a tea garden in Assam from a Southern state expressed his distress about this 'accidental posting' in Assam. He would have preferred to stay down South, he said, and that he was still negotiating with the company to shorten his tenure here in the Northeast. I wasn't the first to ask him questions; his other garden peers, two of whom were Assamese themselves, were the first to start.

What in particular was his problem? he was asked. With the insurgency scare, he didn't want to die by extortion or in bomb blasts, he replied. 'Our Officer sir here can tell us more about where we really stand in terms of safety,' he said, raising his glass at me. I smiled.

Didn't have to answer as his peers, the ones from Assam, went on. 'No, that's not all that happens in Assam, sir. Just being here does not guarantee you violence. Sorry, sir, but this is a wrong assumption,' one of them replied, who I had come to find was a private owner of a tea estate that was established during British rule and handed down to subsequent generations of his family. 'Arre, what you saying, sir, just a few years ago someone from our company was abducted...' The conversation, I assume, went on for a while. I had promptly removed myself from the group. Even after all these years, I am still perplexed by having to fit insurgency and counter-insurgency on two opposite sides of the line. Neatly. Compartmentalised. Certainly not my cup of tea during a casual dinner and drinks...

With time, the gap between the readings lengthened. As much as she hated to accept it, she couldn't quite find something coherent to hold on to. Many weeks had passed since the night she had resolved to embark upon a search for signs across his journals. School picked up. Friends and conversations followed. She began finding solace in literature that exposed her to people with experiences similar to hers. Fictitious characters from books managed to hold her, calm her, excite her and carry her through like a friend. Another friend outside of her books was Rohit, who kept in touch, but only as a friend. She felt less angry at Amma, even though it stung to think of her silence on the day she was barred by her relatives from going to the cemetery. She would go to his grave in her own right someday, when she had made something of herself. When the many other battles that lay before her were won. This one, she chose to sit out. For now.

It went without saying that her father had lived a life of umpteen experiences, a spectrum that could easily transition from exhilarating to morbid. They were available and accessible to her in bits and pieces. through his journals. She loved reading them, for sure, and also cringed at the thought of the crime she was committing; going through his most intimate leftovers without his permission. But she was sure he didn't mind.

Her interest in them slowly shifted in meaning. She read to peek into a part of his life she didn't have access to while he was alive. Some of the entries, like the ones on his experience with insurgency in the 90s, shook her. She was stunned at the thought of just how sheltered her life had been. While so much violence tainted people's everyday lives, she only remembered boat rides across the Baghbor river, spotting a river dolphin for the first in her life with her father beside her, his thrill more childlike than hers. How parents managed to shield their children from a harsh world while living double lives themselves baffled her.

Some memories from those difficult times were still vivid. The frequent army searches on highways, spots around towns dotted with soldiers armed with AK-47's and the near-obligatory curfews during Independence and Republic Day. Once she left for boarding school, these things ebbed away from her everyday existence and also from her mind. Now, post the new millennium, things evidently appeared to have changed. At least in Guwahati city, it was as if those memories from the 90s had been obliterated by the new lived realities of eateries and shopping complexes.

Sara felt sure that it wasn't wise for her to dwell on the past but rather look forward to the future; her future. With her board exams around the corner, she now spent most of her time studying. This was her shot towards the first step she needed to take to keep her promise to Abba. She had to make it to a good college. History, Sociology and Political Science took precedence over anything else. Although it was much rarer, she still flipped through a page or two of the journals, which had become a fictional saga she sought to escape other, more pressing matters.

A lot could change over a decade. Wars could be won and lost, regimes toppled, climate changed, technology amplified, species wiped out, population expanded—the list could go on. People could change, their situations and circumstances waxing and waning like the moon, bringing in different phases of their lives, sometimes for the better and sometimes for the worse. For Sara, the decade passed through several shifts and turns. From finishing college at the top of her class to finding herself without opportunities for the next few years, to witnessing more death within close circles and finding pathways to new countries and people. The incredible dynamism that she suffered and gained from in the past decade brought her closer to only one true maxim in life; that it is random. There are no set patterns and definitely no pre-ordained signs. People move ahead as each day replaces the next, bringing with it possibilities as well as stalemates. There is no staircase building itself exactly the way one would like, leading them to a timeline of their desire, to a place they want to be at. There are no mystical build ups, no esoteric justifications for life's arbitrary incidents, something she once vehemently believed in. Instead, life now represented for her a vast ocean of random waves. One has to choose which ones to ride. Sometimes, we don't even get that choice and the waves are simply thrust upon us. What we do then, is begin to own it. The way she had, with the shifting realities of her own life. When after all her efforts and hard work, her Plan As failed to take shape, she decided to nurture her Plan Bs and was surprised to discover how the Bs were indeed the As all along. That is how life worked.

For Sara, Guwahati had become a getaway. The place she went to in between her life. A life which was now largely away from where her father lay. Her Plan Bs led her towards a career in a sector which allowed her to sustain herself as well as enjoy multicultural experiences. As she grew in years, she felt convinced that the adventures of life could be not be had with roots but with wings, a realisation not afforded to her father by life itself. The further the wings took her, the further she felt from the bitterness she had harboured for so many years about the wrongs that were done to her. It got easier to keep aside the vow she had made of visiting her father's grave once she *arrived* in life, as she was still wandering and wasn't sure what would qualify as having *arrived*. Every time she went home, different elements of her life took precedence over the need to be constantly mindful of her father's last resting place.

She would enjoy the calm comfort of home and the newfound closeness to Amma, owing to a gradual change in her mother's demeanour over the years. She had become much more relaxed and expressive than when Sara was a teenager.

As the years went by, driving past the cemetery where Abba lay became just another crossing; she would even forget to look in his direction and say a silent prayer, something she used to do in the initial years of his passing. Somewhere, she had internalised that she was closest to her father not when she was in proximity with his last resting place but when she began to embody his beliefs as she moved through life—that laughter brought people closer together; love needed expression not concealment; kindness never went unrewarded; new worlds could be discovered in books; one's own company could be terribly enjoyable.

Most importantly, always being a beacon of dependability for one's family, no matter what it took away sometimes.

Sara was home for a few days, on leave for the wedding of one of her closest friends from high school. She was thrilled that the wedding dates happened to fall over a weekend, since they wouldn't count as formal leaves, and she could stay longer. Of late she was not in the best of health, owing to her sedentary work life, and was therefore determined to continue her morning runs even from home. Much to her dismay, she could never manage to wake up at an appropriate time for a run. She had Amma's indulgent dinners to blame for it! Tomorrow, she decided, she would wake up at 5 am no matter what. She managed 5.30.

As she groggily trotted around, crossing deserted streets, passing people standing outside their homes with toothbrushes dangling from their mouths and old ladies setting up tea shops, she suddenly came to a halt. Something struck her and she looked at her watch. 6 am. She looked around. No signs of an auto or cycle rickshaw yet. She jogged ahead to a slightly busier street and found two autos taking their spot in the auto stand which they would claim as theirs for the day. *Ulubari Kabarstan*, she said, hopping on. Her excitement grew with each mile they crossed and she eventually found herself standing in front of the main gate of the cemetery where Abba was. It only took fifteen minutes to get there, courtesy of the empty early-morning roads. She looked around and saw that the slum dwellers around the cemetery were still inside their houses.

She looked at the cemetery caretaker's quarters. No one. She walked ahead, snippets of memories coming back to her from the one time she had tried to come here on her own in a moment of weakness while on a break from college, and was thrown out by the caretakers. 'Women are not allowed. We will call the authorities,' they had said.

Now, as she walked closer to the inner iron gate beyond which her father rested, she felt free of any bitterness or pain. Instead, she found herself smiling. She knew she had to be quick, lest the caretaker saw her and caused trouble. When she reached the rust-infested iron gate, she peeped inside and was dumbfounded.

A huge Ezar tree hovered over Abba's grave, branches laden with bright purple flowers gently sloping towards where he lay. There were fallen flowers all over his grave, covering it like a purple blanket, covering *him*. Abba's Ezar tree. Countless thoughts flooded her in that moment. She saw her teenage self with puffy, tear-soaked eyes, reading her father's journals for answers. Flashes, no, *sounds* of excerpts rang in her head; Abba's voice narrating how it would slightly sting that the Ezars he planted could never be enjoyed by him. Him reciting a poem about the beauty of the Ezar written by an Assamese poet, how he loved the tree's ability to add beauty to whatever it touched. She wiped her eyes, purple vision becoming cloudy, her tears turning the scene into a hazy blur.

As she walked away from the grave, she remembered a girl who used to look for signs. A girl who believed that the universe constantly sent mystical signs to people to help them make sense of life. She remembered the pain behind her search, an inquiry that led her to unintended paths. Paths that eventually helped her take care of that version of herself, and transition into someone who loved life as it came to her.

Sometimes, some versions come back, reminding us of who we used to be. Like this moment, when the signs blazed bright and clear that Abba did get to witness the Ezar bloom, but from an entirely different dimension. The past version of Sara took solace in that. And it was truly alright.

Animal Instinct (2004)

How can the same egg taste so utterly different in two different styles—an omelette versus a sunny side-up? Daisy wondered, recalling the disgust she had felt during breakfast a couple of hours ago, when an omelette was served to her despite being informed of her preference for sunny-side ups. Ideally, nothing short of a strong rebuke to the serving staff would have satisfied her, but on this day, she chose silence. She wanted to avoid coming across as a foul-tempered Delhi University girl before the circuit house staff. It was largely because she didn't want the staff telling on her rude behaviour to her uncle, the Deputy Commissioner of Karbi Anglong district, who had graciously arranged for her stay at this particular government lodging facility at minimal charges so she could easily conduct her research work. He had been kind enough to arrange not only her accommodation but also a car and a driver for the entire duration of her stay, which was nearly a month. A paradisiacal arrangement for any academic researcher. It's no secret how glamorously tiny the university grants for researchers in the Indian academic ecosystem usually were. For the social sciences in particular, if financial support were to be pictorially depicted, it would look like an elephant perched atop the head of a mouse on one foot. The mouse, of course, represents the stipend while the elephant would be the body of work expected of a social-science researcher. Like Daisy. Therefore, an egg-related offence could easily be given a pass, although the hunger pangs in her belly on account of a half-eaten breakfast made her irate. Given that she was on a five-hour-long journey to Jorhat Airport, this was a definite problem. She decided to ask the driver about nearby roadside eateries as a solution.

'Amlan, are there any good *dhabas* nearby? I would like to stop for a quick meal,' she asked.

'*Tch tch*, Madam, it's quite early in the morning, not even 8 am yet. They won't be open around this time.'

'Oh God! What time do you think they would open, then?' she continued, with her annoyance now reflecting in her tone.

'Madam, even if we find something, it will only be after we cross the Nambor forest, which we are about to reach in another twenty minutes or so.'

Daisy closed her eyes and gulped some saliva. In that moment, she realised that her annoyance went deeper than that unsolicited omelette or her now-roaring hunger. Her field work was quite shabby and hardly helpful for the next round of discussions with her PhD supervisor who was already giving her a hard time. 'Your progress is unimpressive Daisy' had become a common reprimand of late. How was she to explain to her supervisor that ethnobotany laced with gender studies was not the easiest of topics to follow through on, especially when it took hours for Daisy to get the women she was interviewing to open up to her. Not her, technically; her translator. Somehow Daisy couldn't help but notice an omnipresent suspicion towards her (but not her translator) present in almost all her interviewees while she probed them with questions on the indigenous wild plants and the role the women played in harnessing their medicinal properties. Or maybe, it was all Daisy's imagination. Perhaps it was the obvious language barrier. Sure, she was Assamese and many in Karbi Anglong spoke Assamese apart from the usual Karbi, but somehow, her research winded up at the steps of those in remote villages, yet untouched by *Lingua Assamica*. In fact, it was quite naïve, if not kind of condescending on Daisy's part to assume that everyone in Assam would speak Assamese.

Grrr. Daisy's stomach growled loudly. Her face flushed pink with embarrassment. She bit her lip, mortified that her driver had obviously heard the disagreeable sound. She began fumbling for something, *anything* in her handbag so the moment would pass but Amlan interrupted her with a question.

'Madam, where are you studying?'

Daisy groaned inwardly. She had forgotten that Amlan was a new driver who had been assigned to her that morning for the airport drop as her regular driver had to attend to some official duty. This change for Daisy meant, shudder, *small talk*. Daisy wished more than anything that her vibe was steely and cold like some of the girls at her university. It was bizarre how scary it was to even think of saying hello to them despite crossing them in the corridors almost every single day. Daisy had no such exterior and she was fully aware that people found it easy to approach her. Too easy. This has to change, she thought as she replied, 'Delhi University.'

'Aah, *baah baah,* Madam, so good, so good.'

'Where is your home in Assam, where do your parents live?' he continued in the same breath.

Mentally letting out another groan, Daisy continued, 'My mother and father are both from Golaghat district in Upper Assam. But I was raised in Guwahati all along since they moved there before my birth. So I guess I could say that I am from Guwahati and my parents live there as well,' she concluded.

'*Borhiya*, very good, big city madam,' Amlan replied, chuckling to himself.

This irked Daisy a bit. What was with the 'big city madam' and the chuckle! She decided to confront him but just before she could, the car suddenly came to a halt in the middle of the road. Before she could enquire further, she noticed that there was a long line of cars ahead of theirs, so at least that ruled out any foul play on Amlan's part. Or did it? She looked around, and was spooked by the canopy formed by the dense trees, almost impregnable against the sunlight. The long, straight road in the middle of the forest resembled a neat hair parting on a woman with dark tresses, long and thick. The foliage was deep green with spurts of light and flecks of yellow, with the air as fresh as the scenery. Somewhere in the distance a cuckoo sang, lending a misplaced sense of lightness to the heavy, thickset scenery. She checked her watch. It was 8 am in summertime. Yet she was enveloped by an eerie, dusky darkness.

She probed Amlan, 'Why have we stopped here?'

'Oh, Madam, it is because of the elephants. They will be passing by in a while.' Daisy was taken aback by this unexpected response.

'Elephants? How do you know?'

'Madam, you see all these vehicles lined up? The Forest Department people come up to these highways when elephants are about to cross over and tell the commuters to halt for some time until they pass. This is an elephant corridor.'

Daisy's mind went technicolour for a few seconds. She was both exasperated and bewildered.

'How long does one have to wait here? I mean, usually?' she added, realising the stupidity of her first question. As if there was a determined time slot for wild elephant crossings.

'It depends, Madam…sometimes it is a couple of hours, sometimes a few minutes.'

A couple of hours! Damn it. Daisy's mind spiralled as her stomach did a quick somersault.

'Shit, man,' she cursed under her breath, unscrewing the Coca-Cola bottle still lying in the car from her last field trip a couple of days earlier. She took a few long swigs, as if trying to drink in life itself. The flat, fizz-less, sugary liquid tasted like medicine. It was infuriating.

'Madam, this is the least of the inconveniences caused by these bastards, I tell you.' Amlan added suddenly. He saw Daisy's frustrated face in the rear-view mirror and decided that bitching about the stressor would diminish its power.

Ignoring her silence, he went on, 'I tell you, Madam, these beasts have destroyed my whole village. Time and again, they come in herds and destroy our crops, trample our houses, our people and whatnot! My woman's father was crushed by a crazed elephant two years ago. His face turned into a *pitha*. What a horrible sight that was. No one thought he would meet such an end. It's true, the old rascal was a drunk. Always telling his wife that a water fairy lived in the depths of their backyard pond and kept beckoning him to bathe with her. He blabbered on about this for more than two years. My woman and I live near their house and I used to be called by his frantic wife so many times to pull him back to the house from the edge of the pond. I was fully convinced that the pond would be the end of him. But the funny thing in this whole situation is that it was a drunk who killed another drunk. Can you believe it, Madam? My father-in-law was smashed to pulp by a drunk elephant whilst he was drunk himself. How strange is fate. *Tch tch…*' Amlan trailed off into thought towards the end of his long and informative monologue to the madam.

Daisy, who was by now fully resigned to the idea that this was an ill-fated day, could feel curiosity starting to latch onto her growling stomach, like algae does on walls, for the situation she found herself in was a first for her. While growing up in Assam, she had mostly been bound to the city. Her brushes with wilderness had been limited to school excursions to wildlife sanctuaries or passing by Kaziranga National Park enroute upper Assam where she used to visit her grandparents during some vacation or the other. To be stranded in the middle of a forest and awaiting a herd of wild elephants to pass by was unplanned, unanticipated and a bit thrilling. To top it up, being at the receiving end of a tale where a drunk elephant kills a drunk man was a promising window to an entirely different world which she was getting an opportunity to peek into. She only wished she had medium fries and a cheesy double-decker chicken burger to go with it.

'What do you mean by a drunk elephant?' She questions Amlan, completely intrigued.

'What? You have never heard of drunk elephants? That is common knowledge, Madam. These giant bastards have a huge weakness for the local brew, and will stop at nothing to get a sip of it. They can trample a mountain…no, Mount Everest itself for a few swigs…the drunks that they are.'

'How do they get access to alcohol? And what alcohol?'

'The local alcohol, Madam, that gets brewed in some of the houses in the village. Some communities make rice beer and keep it in their homes. Once a passing herd gets a whiff of it, they keep coming back. No invitation required. Self-invitation and destruction.'

'Hah!' Daisy chuckled. 'Wow, drunk elephants!' she muttered to herself, craning her neck, torso dangling out the window, to count the number of cars ahead of hers. Four.

'Why "wow", Madam?' Amlan interjected after a brief pause, sounding solemn and almost hurt as he asked the question.

Before Daisy could respond, he continued. 'It is not very amusing to see beasts destroy lives and livelihoods, Madam.

Do you have any idea how many people have died in my own village under their feet? Just last year alone, there were no less than a dozen deaths. Children left without fathers and mothers, even children themselves squashed to death, in many instances. Most of us in the village are farmers, Madam, and we toil very hard on our crops. Elephants come in, fully entitled, as if they own everything they see before them, and just go on a rampage. Who will take responsibility, Madam? The government? Hah! They promise compensation to the families of those that are killed by elephants. But do you know how long it takes for those families to actually see that money? I don't see God helping either. If he would have, then some disease would have afflicted these creatures and wiped them off the earth, like dinosaurs. And good riddance, it would've been. I wonder how poachers are not going after them at the same rate as the rhinos. But don't worry, Madam. As neither the government nor God have come to our aid, we have taken matters in our own hands and have become experts in making delicious poison for the beasts. When that fails, we make sure to charge our fences real good. Let those beasts fry.' Amlan was smiling to himself as he finished, his solemn mood at the start capsized and replaced with something amusing, as if reminiscing about a scene from one such episode of 'beast frying'.

Daisy found this jarring for several reasons. First, her own lack of knowledge on drunk elephants. Second, the hurt in Amlan's voice at the beginning, which she did not want to take responsibility for. Third, the obvious enormity of the conflict between humans and elephants in her state that she was not very attuned to. Fourth, the ease with which her driver conveyed his spite and death-wish for the entire species. And finally, the solutions that his people had adopted. She was, after all, an educated, cultured woman of the world, and compassion for the co-inhabitants of the planet was a very natural instinct to have for someone like her.

She found the summary rejection of an entire species for what appeared to be the fault of a handful to be regressive, uncouth and simply unacceptable. She decided to do what most educated people are expected to do; *correct* the uneducated.

'I don't think it's very nice of you to say that, Amlan. Have you ever considered that maybe *we* are the problem, not them? We are to blame for the pressures we have created in their lives and that's why they behave the way they do? If we hadn't taken over their homes, their habitats, would they feel the need to come to ours?'

'What pressures are we creating, Madam? We have remained in our villages; we have not moved even an inch here or there. It has been like this since the time of our forefathers. We don't go into their homes, their forests and burn everything down. Why do they come to ours?' Amlan retorted scornfully.

At this point, Daisy straightened up on her seat, as she sometimes did back at her university, while taking lessons for the graduate students as part of her PhD requirement. As someone who had already gone through the motions of higher education, graduate students seemed half-baked to her, with grandiose self-perceptions about being very informed and cultivated in their subjects. A perception Daisy enjoyed cracking each time she straightened up in her seat and threw a plethora of additional literature their way. In a less intellectual manner, she decided to do the same with Amlan.

'Okay, tell me, Amlan, where is your village situated? In which district?'

'Numaligarh, in Golaghat district.'

'Aha!' Daisy almost jumped in her seat, as if she had found the cure to cancer.

'This makes perfect sense now,' she continued. 'You see, Amlan, where your village is situated also happens to be a place with an oil refinery. When such mega structures come up and replace forests, where do you think its inhabitants will go? Obviously to villages like yours. Elephants need their corridors, so when what used to be their corridors becomes enmeshed in oil pipes, they make forays into adjoining areas, villages and such, forging new corridors. Can you see things through their eyes, Amlan?' With the last sentence, her voice tapered down like a kindergarten teacher trying to emphasise the non-edibility of chalk to a pupil.

'Of course we know everything you just said. We may not be educated at Delhi University but we are not stupid, Madam.' Amlan responded with controlled but obvious irritation. 'That does not mean we sit like ducks and watch as they flatten our children, homes and income sources, does it?'

'Hey, not all of them kill people, I know that for a fact.' Ignoring the spite in his tone, she continued. 'It is usually a lone bull. And not—'

'Madam, this is what you are not understanding!' Amlan interrupted before Daisy could finish her last sentence. 'Whether it is a lone bull or a herd of murderers, we are still suffering under their feet and who is going answer for it? Mother Nature does not speak any language, so certainly not her.'

'Language was an invention of idiocy and not intelligence. A manifestation of our instinctual weakness, unlike that of several of the universe's creations.'

'What, Madam?' Not a single word that had been uttered by the madam could be apprehended, so Amlan stuck to his first response.

'Never mind.' Daisy said. What was she thinking, really? Rambling on about the universe's creations and semantics to Amlan. Sometimes she did things like that. Speaking to herself more than the other person.

Seeing that the conversation was going nowhere, Daisy decided to drop the subject. It was obviously a futile exercise, trying to enter the precarious space of human–animal conflict, especially on this one, peculiar drive. It takes years for conservation organizations to strike a chord with people like Amlan to safeguard the endangered, for the simple fact that it is our duty to do so. She was simply wasting her breath trying to get him to agree in one conversation, that too under the current circumstances. Yet, seeing such deeply rooted anger among what she assumed to be thousands of people, if not more, was very concerning.

This was a battle for some other time, if she ever wished to enter this particular battlefield; that is. For now, her immediate fight was the hunger in her stomach which had by now crawled up to her pituitary gland. She leaned her head back on the seat, put on her headphones and a number from her 80's rock collection, and closed her eyes in the hopes of distracting herself for a while. She quickly fell into a slumber.

'Madam, Madam…Madam,' the repeated calls finally perforated through a Metallica riff, so Daisy removed the headphones and opened her eyes to respond to this oft menacing yet magnificent world. As intended, her nap had been a power nap, so she felt as fresh as her name despite the ache in her stomach birthed from the unattended hunger. As her eyes retrieved focus, she noticed something big and grey lurking next to Amlan's window.

She froze.

An elephant was standing right next to their car. The head and upper torso weren't visible from where she sat with a rapidly quickening heartbeat. As she gaped at the proximity of the giant to her car and to herself, she noticed the trunk swaying breezily like a light symphony, undecided whether its melody needed to break free and sneak into the slightly open car window. This was hardly a first encounter for Daisy. She was, after all, a resident of a country where it was neither abnormal nor extraordinary to witness cars, buses, motorcycles, scooters, bicycles, rickshaws, pedestrians, cows, dogs and sometimes an elephant guided by its *mahaot* in a traffic jam. But this felt different. It seemed like the elephant's actions were fully intentional, and it was completely in command of itself with no iron rod prodding it to move. Instead, it had moved towards the car, towards Amlan, towards Daisy—entirely of its own accord. Like there was something to say, an exchange to be made, a language which was being relayed. Everyone was an idiot; this was inter-species idiocy.

As Daisy's mind meandered across such thoughts, up popped the intrusive image of her arm being wrung out of her body by a deathly twist of the beast's trunk. Suddenly, her body went frigid, but her eyes followed the grey in the periphery and fixed themselves on Amlan. The sight being observed was wholly and utterly unbelievable for the observer.

With complete calmness, Amlan stooped below and retrieved a stack of bananas from the bottom of the passenger seat. He then turned his body slightly towards the window, joined his hands together and muttered a short, indecipherable prayer under his breath after which he rolled down the window. The trunk came in with a well-practised move. As the stack of bananas were placed in the hollow of the trunk, it withdrew, pushing the offering deep into a dark hole beneath it. The elephant slowly turned and moved away to join the rest of its peers, many of whom stood by restaurant windows of their own preferences, some citric, some sweet, some grassy. As the herd came back into a singular formation to continue their journey, the car ignition was turned on.

Daisy wondered why she hadn't been offered at least one out of the dozen bananas that had been hidden beneath the passenger seat this whole time.

Love is a Flimsy Kite (2019)

'Hey...'

'Hi...'

Pause.

Breaking the silence, he asks, 'So, you bunking?'

She responds, 'No way! Just here for some water. Ms Demand-Supply is way too strict. She scrutinises the attendance register before starting every class.'

No response. That's it?

'I don't know how you all study social science...so much mugging up, so much writing...my head spins from just thinking about it.'

So it continues. A slow warmth creeps across her cheeks.

'Huh! There is no mugging *shugging,* please...especially in Economics. One has to understand the concepts, draw the relations.'

'Hmmm, maybe...' he mumbles, hands tucked in his pockets, feet making unnecessary patterns with the slight pool of water that had gathered outside the girls' and boys' toilets. She forbids her mind from trying to decipher the source of this water. Yuck.

'Are you liking this school?' She probes.

Both of them were newcomers in the 11th grade, after having completed their tenth from other schools. They were standing together on one side of the line, wanting to cross over to the other with hopes of new friendships, new epitaphs. Epitaphs that were rewritten with words that embellished the lives of seventeen-year-olds in the new millennium—*cool, chill, dope, bro, guys, gals.*

'Yeah…I guess it's okay, not good, not bad,' he replies. 'It's only been a month so there is more to find out, I guess.'

How elusive. What an annoying trait, she thinks. *What's with all the 'guessing'? If only his answers had a bit more depth, like the dimple on his left cheek.*

'I am beginning to like it. At least I get to go home in the afternoon unlike my previous boarding school. Finding parts of my girl gang too. I like how I'm vibing here.' She goes on, giving in to her trademark long-winded replies to questions often unasked.

'Hey, the bell is about to go off and I don't want to be caught bunking another period. Guess I'll see you later then,' he waves a vague goodbye with his right hand while the left buries itself deeper into the pockets of his ill-fitting pants as he makes a dash for the classroom.

'Y-yeah, sure,' she fumbles her response, her face suddenly hot with a mixture of embarrassment and ignominy. As she rushes back to the last of Ms Demand-Supply for the day, she wonders whether the guy she has had her eyes on since the first day of the new school would actually see her later or if she has simply been snubbed.

'Adore your hair. Promise to never straighten it,' he whispers to her as they lay spooning, her back facing him while he props himself up on one elbow and plays with her curls with his free hand. She smiles with her eyes closed. Distant words ring in her ears—*llama, Maggi, pubes on the head*. She has to learn to receive compliments about her thick, unruly curly hair from her lover without doubting them. It takes time to accept, let alone love the physical features that earned you your childhood nicknames and helped kickstart the careers of bullies. Those very features are now surrendered, coyly yet surely to an entirely different, delicious scrutiny.

They have just made love for the very first time. It has taken them a month to get here. They are both bound by the hostel timings of their respective colleges. No private places to meet, to explore each other's bodies in leisure. She had fought fiercely with her family to allow her an apartment with two of her friends. 'My friends' parents trust them and treat them like adults, which we all are! Why can't you treat me the same?' she had shouted at her parents through tears when they categorically stated that if she wanted to study in Delhi University, she would have to take up residence at the college hostel and abide by the rules. Or else, they were happy to have her attend college from home in Guwahati. She had given in finally, clinging to the reassuring knowledge that he had gotten into a Delhi college too. It was better to be together in the same city than apart. Any day. She could always figure out the privacy issue later. Indeed, this problem was solved quickly enough, with several friends generously offering their apartments to the lovers.

The act of sex did not feel the way she had thought it would. A little pain, a handful of awkward movements and a strange sense of completion at the end. It was not the sheer chemistry that their make-out sessions behind the cafeteria in their school used to be. After their first short encounter near the filthy toilets, they became fast friends. Despite being from two different streams and hence in separate classes, they waited for each other during recess and after school. Soon, the teasing began and what was already present between the two was sealed with a quick kiss on the backseat of the school bus one afternoon after everyone else had left. From then on, classes were intelligently bunked—not-so-important ones for her, like Physical Education, and very important ones for him, like Physics practicals and Biology—to spend hours snogging in a secret clearing they had discovered behind the school cafeteria. The intensity of their physical romance deepened through the two years of high school, although stopping short of crossing a certain line.

Until today. It all feels so comfortable. Wrapped around her best friend, her confidante, the one who knows everything there is to know about her. Even the dark birth mark spread out like a confused constellation around her groin area; the one she has always despised and feared exposing to her lover. He makes no remarks on it.

'I love you.'

'I love you too.'

'Happy fourth anniversary, my love,' she texts him. A mild but persistent gnawing feeling lurks around her temples as she does. Has she done the right thing by coming on this college trip on the day of their anniversary? Maybe not. They should have been together on this day. However, as she reasons with herself again, she had missed her first college trip the year before, the one that had been organised by the Department of Political Science. Instead, she had gone with him on a trip up north to the splendid hills, while informing her parents that she would be out of network coverage on account of her college trip far away from Delhi. She does sly things like these. She has to. It was their first couple's getaway without a care in the world. Oh, how she revelled in the newness of it all.

From budgeting with their pocket money, to the overnight bus journey and midnight snacking at a highway *dhaba,* to booking couple-friendly budget hotels cocooned amidst apple orchards. Despite the thrill of such exhilarating freedom with her lover, she knew she had missed a great bonding opportunity with her classmates by bailing on the actual college trip. So in her second year of college, she chooses differently, sheltered by the years of security with her partner, a relationship that has outlasted famous Hollywood marriages.

Besides, he hardly ever gets *suo moto* upset with her. It's usually her who picks on something and then she prosecutes while he defends, hardly belligerent, using logic over sentiments to counter-argue. 'One seldom gets aggressive with weed, unlike with alcohol. So why not condemn and criminalise drinking and leave the harmless herbalists alone? How often do you hear of families dissolving, domestic violence, vandalism and whatnot due to these herbs?' he says with a grin, when she tries to chastise him for his now-frequent smoking.

Her own thoughts surprise her. She catches herself thinking in legal analogies. Who would have ever expected him to switch from a science background to law! He had never discussed this with her up until the end of their high school when one day, he suddenly declared that he would like to study law.

'Fuck science, fuck medical. I am so done,' he had said.

Frankly, she had been surprised when he managed to score decently in the all-India entrance examination for law, given his meagre inclination towards studying, especially for exams. The cherry on the cake was his selection at a law school in Delhi—glistening ripe and red, pulsating with the promise of an exciting journey of togetherness for the inseparable couple.

She is annoyed right from the moment she enters his dingy room. There is a layer of grime on the floor. The hooks on the wall have been bearing the weight of unwashed denims and T-shirts for months. The so-called study table resembles a marketplace hit by a grenade, with bits of broken stationary strewn all over like severed limbs. A few pens with missing caps, a broken coffee mug-turned-ashtray overflowing with cigarette buds starting to fossilise, two *Rock Street* journals perched on top of each other, the rockstar's face on the cover stained with God knows what and half-covered with leftover marijuana seeds. The battery-operated Chinese table lamp was bent to hover over the *Rock Street* journals, turned far away from the objects that actually needed illumination: his course books, shunned and neatly stacked against the wall to the far left of the 'study table'.

It's three in the afternoon when she enters this glamourous bachelor pad he shares with two other boys from his law school with the spare keys he gave her. She is the only person privileged enough to have the extra keys since the other two dingbats couldn't have conjured girlfriends for themselves even with human sacrifice.

He isn't in his room. She had called him prior to her arrival and he had said he would be back from college by now. Where is he?

The flush…*aha*! He's in the bathroom. Her stomach tightens slightly for some reason. It's either the thought of the algae-like sediments on the corners of the bathroom floor, or the usual suspect—the unconcealable excitement that runs through her at the prospect of seeing him. Even after all these years, despite seeing him almost every day.

'Hey boo, wassup.'

'Nothing much,' she responds, her voice not betraying even half the annoyance she thought it would have picked up by now on seeing the state of dilapidation and decay all around her.

'Wanna catch a movie?'

'Where?'

'Laptop, obviously. Just struck a gold mine of the latest. Let's start an Oscar marathon, yeah?'

She snaps, 'Why do we always have to be locked up in this dark hole of yours? Why can't we just go out for a change?'

She flings her tote bag onto his bed as she makes her way to what can be described as a mini-kitchen. She grabs the bottle of Coke gone flat, taking a large swig from it, although she is actually desperate for some water.

'Why snapping, boo? We do go out. Pork with bamboo shoot dinner just last week at Delhi Haat. This week you said you are busy with your term paper presentation.'

'I am not snapping! Why do you always accuse me this way? Why does everyone only pick on me all the time?' The decibel levels of her voice are rising.

'Okay. Something is very wrong with you. Please tell me what it is. Who is picking on you?' he says, looking straight at her from the bed where he now sits, alert and ready to face her challenges.

'For starters, you! And my professor, my classmates, everyone!' She slouches on the chair opposite the bed and leans back, the back of her hand covering her eyes.

'The first part, untrue. For the rest, come on, spill. You know I can listen,' he says carefully, as he takes both his hands to her lap and starts stroking her thighs gently.

'I don't know, man…why is this bothering me so much…' she begins. 'I felt so personally attacked while defending my term paper. Those fucking idiots and their leader. He could have steered the discussion more sensibly. They are all in cahoots.'

'Hmmm…a little more specificity would help here.'

'You know how for my term paper, I picked Assam's Bengali-speaking Muslims as my case study? I tried to draw on their historical mobility, their arrival to the Brahmaputra valley from the Bengal districts of colonial Assam and how today, their progeny find themselves critically threatened due to the political formulations of the last few decades.'

'Critically threatened? Like our rhinos?' He chuckles.

'Please be serious. Why would these cultivators just randomly appear from Mymensingh to the Brahmaputra valley if not for the British coaxing them out of there for their self-interests? The colonisers literally depended on these Mymensinghia cultivators to turn swathes and swathes of wastelands into productive agrarian assets for the empire. Wherever an indigenous cultivator left an inch of land fallow, the Mymensinghia moved in to make it fertile. And today, their progeny has to live under the perennial threat of being sent to detention centres for their inability to show papers!'

Silence.

'What? No reaction?' She presses on, the boundary lines of her manufactured calm beginning to smudge.

'*Arre baba*, I am listening. So yes, what happened then? Why are you upset with your professor and classmates?'

'You won't believe what that right-wing fascist Aniruddha said. During the fifteen minutes of Q&A, it was mostly us arguing. He started with how my paper then "postulates" that citizenship should be loosely defined and aliens should enjoy all rights and privileges afforded to a legal Indian citizen with complete impunity from the State. And as an extension of that logic, we, the Assamese, shouldn't have a problem with the hordes of illegal Bangladeshi immigrants pushing us out of our own lands. He made this statement, that moron, flashed his ugly crooked teeth at me and just left it at that. No valid question asked, just a statement hurled at me, waiting for me to wipe the dirty smear of his words from my face.'

'How did you respond?'

'The only correct way. I clarified that anyone aspiring to be a political scientist should be intellectually capacitated to understand the difference between "illegal aliens" and internally displaced people. I clarified that the subject population of my paper clearly refers to those Bengali-speaking Muslims whose ancestors migrated to the Brahmaputra valley from a British province itself, way before the thought of a Bangladesh took root in people's minds, let alone after its creation.'

'And then?'

'And then what? He continued with his weak and biased counter arguments while the sorry ass of a professor refused to mediate or intervene. I think he took some sadistic pleasure, given how he is known to wear his khaki shorts for his brisk morning walks by the ridge, enticing the monkeys along the fence to ogle at his jiggling, hairy thighs.'

'My God, you are savage. I feel like I should cover my thighs now. As you can see, might attract them monkeys,' He gestures towards his thighs exaggeratedly while suppressing a grin.

The mood is lightened. She smiles to herself, amused by her own words.

'But I am serious,' she continues, while climbing onto the slightly shaky single bed, making for the comforting depths of his broad chest and sinewy arms and the lingering smell of Axe Chocolate, sweat and cigarettes that she has grown to fawn over. 'The professor could have steered the Q&A to a more progressive direction but he chose to leave me in the middle of the ring and let loose a band of hungry bloodhounds. Oh, but I gave it back, I tell you. It's too long and I don't want to get into the details but wait…you just HAVE to hear the question that Madam Gracey asked. She was like, "What would your state have to say about its Islamisation, given that there will be more Muslims there than any other community at this rate?" Can you believe her? Bitch.'

Silence.

'Isn't Grace your good friend? I thought you both hang out a lot,' he asks, his expression turning a bit serious.

'Hey, going clubbing twice a year with someone, that too in a gang, doesn't necessarily make two people close,' she retorts, her ponytail swinging from side to side.

'Hmmm.'

'What hmmm? Don't you have anything to say?'

'Nope.'

'Your nope sounds fake. Why did you say it that way?'

'What way?'

'You know what way. It doesn't sound like a genuine nope.'

'My God, how do you come up with all this? A nope is a nope. Simple. Straight. How can a nope sound different to what it is supposed to sound like? Nope.'

'Holy shit! Are you insinuating that Grace was correct? You usually have things to say about such stuff but your silence today looks like you're complicit.'

'Complicit! Isn't this an unnecessary word? Complicit in what?'

'In the crime of supporting all these prejudices! Are you blind to all the criminal, fascist presuppositions in the things I just told you? Everything I narrated reflects unconcealed Islamophobia.'

'Boo, you're not the only Muslim here, so am I...but I must say...I think you are overthinking this. There is a genuine concern for the state, with the uninhibited population spurt of the *Miyas*. If unchecked, there will actually be no space left for the indigenous people, which includes us even. So to call a spade a spade is not really a crime. It's stating a fact as it is.'

'Fact?' she sniggers. 'Since we're talking facts here, can you please elaborate on the "us" that you just mentioned? By "us", do you mean the so-called indigenous Muslims from Upper Assam, or is this "us" kind enough to encompass the likes of *my* family too, who speak Bengali, and whose ancestors came to the valley from Sylhet? As far as I am concerned, the word *Miya* applies to people like my family. So your "us" is not really as inclusive as you are trying to make it sound. And this, right here, is a fact, Your Honour.' She is heaving as she finishes.

It isn't his nature to push a heated situation. Hell, he would withdraw at the hint of emerging heat, let alone lead a situation towards a meltdown. He hates confrontations, face-offs, abetting any complicated discussions. It is ironic, in fact, that he chose to study law, given this intrinsic nature of his. A man of contradictions. But this time, he wants to continue; he wants to push for the logical to replace the illogical, to talk some sense into her. So he continues. 'By us, I meant those who assimilated well, which includes, in your words, the "likes of your family". Your family, irrespective of their origins, gentrified itself, adopted the language and integrated with the class strata, with more than half its members being either in public services or in academia. I hope you're getting what I'm trying to say here.'

She stares at him coldly throughout his narration, as if seeing something for the first time. As he stops to ask if she understands what he is trying to say, she responds calmly, 'Is fuck you gentrified enough?'

She then grabs her bag and dashes out of the house.

Fairy lights enhance any place, she thinks as she walks into her classmate Johann's apartment. Such a difficult apartment to find, located as it is in a decrepit corner of Vijay Nagar—the bad side, not the posh side. Cheap housing here for Delhi University students meant wall-less staircases leading to rooftop apartments, *nay*, rooms with chipped, moldy walls. The saving grace was usually the easy access to the terraces. It is here, on Johann's terrace, that the after-party for the Political Science batch of 2015 is being hosted. The formal graduation dinner in the college premises had concluded at a decent 9 pm. Now, most of the formal, traditional attires have been replaced with tank tops, shorts, dresses, racer-backs and even pajamas, for the chill scenes on Johann's terrace. Fairy lights adorn the entire terrace, hanging from wall to wall like synapses, even from the rope that usually holds laundry and dirty underwear on non-party days. It is hot and dry, Delhi being Delhi in June. This evening though, the effect of the mind-numbing loo is somewhat diminished. Perhaps it is the effect of the sundowner, or a parting gift from the Delhi weather gods to this bunch of young adults which has had their fair share of suffering the infamous, merciless Delhi summer for three straight years. A light breeze is blowing ever so slightly, compounding the merry effects of the Malana weed specially brought in from Kasaul to augment the last of celebrations.

She is here with him. By now they have common friends despite being from different colleges and the *ganja* gang within her friend circle have struck up a solid camaraderie with him over the last few years. They have all pooled in money for the party. Of course, there would be a few freeloaders in the crowd. But all is forgiven tonight. Cheap beer bottles float in messy ice buckets. The fridge is manifestly inadequate to hold all these bottles.

The thing about Delhi, though, is that there will always be arrangements for all and sundry. For the elites, there are posh areas ensconced within medieval monuments where a beer costs thrice its market price, and full plates of kebabs, although soft and succulent, are portioned for mice. A well-designed ploy to keep the tab running, maybe.

Diametrically opposite are the very many lanes both in the old and new *gallis* of the same city where cauldrons deep fry everything, from white bread to meat-balls and of course, the omnipresent momos. The larger-than-life iron skillets that serve a multitude of stuffed *paranthas* for college-going wallets stuff the bellies of the likes of Johann and gang and also the nouveau riche of this astonishingly diverse city.

Today, for the party, the menu exhibits a wide array of snack choices from the *desi* Chinese outlets that dot the university campus. Their secret to success is not really a secret; cheap prices and big portions. A direct hit for the average college-goer. She cannot get enough of the fried schezwan chicken momos lying in heaps atop a study table. Never mind that they are soggy and cold at the moment. Besides, three beers and three vodka shots down, who the hell cares!

The rooftop apartment has two rooms: one bedroom and the other resembling more of a storage space. The presence of a single bed with a psychedelic bedsheet is what lends it the privilege of being called the second room. It is on this bed that the two of them are lounging now. It's 1 am. The party rages on outside with the speakers blasting club music and enticing the crowd to endless rounds of drinking and dancing. Dirty dancing. Some new couples seem to have emerged on the dance floor, grinding on each other to the latest RnB tunes; the host has his tongue tied up with a college junior, the only one from the junior batch to be invited for obvious reasons. A girl is throwing up in the only flower pot in one of the corners; the *ganja* gang is huddled in a sacred circle of their own, being serenaded by a boxer-clad, *desi* Bob Dylan in sunglasses.

These two have broken off from the crowd and are wrapped in each other's arms on the psychedelic bed with leaves and vine prints glowing neon on the sheet. They are both inebriated on the substance of their preference.

'Boo, are you going to miss me?' She opens her eyes to focus on his as she asks, trying her best to give him a look that becomes a core memory for him. She is ambitious even when drunk. He moves closer to her ear while sliding his hand under her top, moving it towards her breasts as he whispers, 'No.'

She kicks him playfully. He laughs out loud. Hugging her close to his chest, he repeats, 'Will I even get a chance to miss you if we'll always be connected? Whatsapp *zindabaad*! Internet *zindabaad*!'

'It's not the same at all, and you know it. I read a blog by some American called Virginia Satire? Or Satir, or something like that, that we need four hugs a day to survive, eight for maintenance and twelve for growth. Can you believe this shit? I do.'

'Then don't go.' Silence.

'You know I have to.' She starts rubbing her eyes frantically as she says this, hoping to get out of her drunken stupor with the conversation getting serious. She starts to break away from his embrace.

He pins her down, his lips coaxing hers to open up to him. He kisses her long and deep and she responds with enthusiasm.

Breaking away slowly, he puts his nose close to hers and whispers, 'I know you have to and I want you to. You deserve it, you are the best.'

She buries her face in his neck. He pulls her face close to his again and says, 'One year will literally fly by. Get your ass back to me right after and I will double all those damn hugs. Until then, don't go hunting for some uber-white British baron.'

'Then we get engaged?'

'Totally. Can't wait to tell my parents I selected a super gorgeous, ultra-smart *Miyani* daughter-in-law for them!'

Grabbing his t-shirt firmly, she looks straight at him and states, 'An Oxford returned *Miyani* daughter-in-law. Aren't they lucky!'

'Yeah, baby! Come here, you…'

An entwinement; shared laughter that returns only as a memory years later, laced with wind chimes and fragrances. A night, a promise; faith and doubt coating snapshots of an intoxicating youth, of moments that hardly ever return. To either one of them.

'So tell me, how was your week?'

'Okay…no great shakes.'

'Any significant change that you noticed in your mood?'

'Hmmm, not sure. I guess on Wednesday, or maybe Thursday, I was a bit low.'

'Could you please elaborate on that?'

'I woke up pretty late, around 10.30 in the morning. Mummy was quite upset. So that upset me further. I skipped breakfast, naturally. Then I did a few things and slept again around two until I somehow heard the *Maghrib azaan* and woke up.'

'Around what time?'

'I guess between 5.30 and 6.'

'Apart from your mother getting upset over you waking up late, was there anything else you can recollect that bothered you?'

Pause.

'Maybe.'

'Can you share what that might be?'

'The night before, I was scrolling through Facebook and I came across something on my feed. There was a post from my ex, a status. He had written something in opposition to the CAB. That sort of triggered me a little, I guess.'

'CAB as in…?'

'The Citizenship Amendment Bill.'

'Oh yes, yes, sorry, didn't register the abbreviation right away. The situation is quite tense in your state at the moment, right?'

'Yes, it's pretty intense. None of us have really gone out of our houses of late. People are out on the streets; vandalism, protest marches and all that jazz that comes with mass uprisings.'

'Sounds like a lot. Getting back to the point... do you mind elaborating on how you felt triggered by your ex's post?'

'You know the whole story. We broke up because he did not want to get married to someone with my background. Someone without "indigenous" roots. Now when the whole state is chanting "no Bangladeshis in Assam, Muslim nor Hindu", it somehow just took me back to my relationship with him.'

Pause.

'Are you there?'

'Yes.'

'Okay, I thought the phone got disconnected for a moment.'

'No, I am here. But see, these are the perils of having telephonic psychotherapy. I am sure if I was sitting in front of you on a couch, you would have scribbled some extra notes upon observing my silence, my dead eyes, the shape my lips formed while speaking those lines, yadda yadda yadda.'

'Haha, perhaps, perhaps, but you are the one who rejected all your local therapists and fished me out, all the way from Bangalore. I do truly believe that one always finds the therapist they need. It's almost mystical. So here we are. We've been doing this over the phone for seven months now and I think you're handling it quite well. This is working out. I want you to know this.'

'True, true. By the way, I thought about what you said the other day; whether I would like to switch to video mode. I think I'll take a rain-check on that. Somehow this feels more comfortable to me.'

'Absolutely fine by me. Whatever works for you. Now, there was no disconnection but I sensed something incomplete in that pause. I feel like you stopped halfway there.'

'We have gone through this topic many times. I don't want to give it more power by discussing it over and over again.'

Pause.

'I understand. But I'd like to encourage you in today's session to try and touch upon it, since you did bring it up as something that bothered you this past week. It is true that we have gone through the topic of your past relationship at length. However, as someone who is trained to observe and understand the human mind and as a consequence, behavioural patterns, I can tell you with full confidence that probing and analysing our triggers are the only ways for us to stop them from being triggers.'

Pause.

'I don't think of him. At all. Every fibre of my being is aware of the fact that that ship has sailed. But I'm still angry. I get mad because I was made to feel less. And somehow, I am still…less.

It's been three years since I completed my Master's and I am still nowhere near where I want to be. I know I told you that I came back to India from England because my student visa ran out but there were many in my situation who managed to turn things around. I did absolutely nothing with the three months that were still left on my visa, and chose to come back home. I could have, *should* have tried for an internship. Maybe that would have opened further doors for me. I don't know where the hell I am going from here. I want to vomit every time I speak to my supervisor at the NGO.'

'You mean the NGO that you are working for at the moment?'

'Yes. I mean, after a Master's degree in Public Policy from the most prestigious institution in the world, I get told that I have poor table setting skills for conferences by a bloody local college graduate! With her bamboo earrings and half-baked hair, she thinks she is the greatest gender expert in Northeast India. Possibly the whole of India! Why is God doing this to me? Why don't I hear back from any of my job applications for Delhi?'

'Alright, we need to take a deep breath and take a few steps back here. You have expressed time and again to me that you are unhappy at your current workplace but also that this is only a temporary stint to gain experience. Isn't that so?'

'Yes. It's been over a year now. It does not feel temporary to me anymore. I am stuck.'

'I beg to differ here. I understand how prolonged dissatisfaction can make one feel stuck in situations but no situation is truly permanent. There is always, always a window. Let's try to look at it this way. When you got back from England, you had some plans in mind for taking the public service examinations. The first two years are accounted for here. Despite the attempts not working out, you have acquired a vast body of knowledge due to your preparations for those exams. You have so many interesting things to share and sometimes you cite facts and figures in our conversations that positively surprise me. Genuinely. So I won't look at those two failed attempts as a waste and should you wish to try again, you know you can. And now, since you have decided to take a break from trying and mobilise your Plan B, which is to be in the NGO sector, you have grabbed an opportunity that has made itself available for now rather than wait for an ideal offer. So much strategy and thought has been applied here. Do you truly feel it's fair to yourself to view these experiences so harshly?'

'But it's taking too much time and I feel like I'm drowning. I failed to stay back in England, I failed to crack the exams and now I am failing at finding a worthy job. And yes, I failed in my personal life. I am alone today while he can't stop pasting pictures of his new girl all over social media. Failure is becoming embossed in all aspects of my life while I just watch.'

'Wow, my dear girl. This is a lot of self-dejection. May I remind you that you are only twenty-five?'

'Twenty-six in two months.'

'Doesn't matter. You are at the precipice here and definitely not the end. Before going into that, let us get back to the triggers we were discussing earlier. I am glad that you brought up the topic of your relationship again, since we were digressing before. Here is what I hope you try and understand. As far as you've told me, the relationship was not very fulfilling for you, at least towards the end. Is that right?'

'Yes, maybe.'

'You have told me over multiple sessions that even during your college years, there were cracks, with you being disappointed over his lack of ambition, drug use and mode of living.'

'Not drug use, marijuana.'

'Still a drug.'

'Alright, if you insist. I was such a fool, you know. Sometimes I think there was a part of me that subconsciously decided to return for him.'

'This is a new strand of thought. You never mentioned this earlier, at least explicitly.'

'Of course…because I am ashamed. Six months into my Master's, we broke up when he said he is not comfortable bringing up the topic of me or our engagement to his parents. Quite openly, he said that his family might object to my background. BACKGROUND! Can you imagine? This is the 21st century. I slammed the phone down and never spoke to him again. There was no closure.'

'I am aware that there was an abrupt end to your conversations, but in our earlier sessions you mentioned that it was the distance that drove a permanent wedge. This is the first time you are revealing this bit about the background. Can I ask why you are sharing this now?'

'A part of me…perhaps the famous feminine instinct, time and again made me aware of that dark spot in the relationship. He would lovingly call me a *Miyani* but I was never comfortable. I was too embarrassed to ever bring it up before him.'

'Why were you embarrassed?' Pause.

'I have absolutely no idea. I am not even sure if embarrassment is the word. Shock, perhaps, that the word would be so loosely used.'

'Do you think the word is derogatory?'

'I don't know. I don't know anything anymore.'

'Okay, I am going to give you some feedback here…'

Acknowledgements

I knew from the moment I finished the first draft of *Colour My Grave Purple*, that the pleasure of crafting this work of love would stop at that point and a long, frustrating journey to the world of publishing would begin. Much to my surprise, the journey was neither too long nor too disappointing, simply because of the magnanimous people the book encountered along the way. My agent, Lalitha Ravindran, was the first person beyond my close friends and family to extend her generosity to this book. Right from the very beginning, her resolute faith in my work ensured that it found a proper channel of expression. Very much a part of my inner circle now, much is owed to this indomitable human being.

I owe my publishers, Niyogi Books, immensely for their conviction that frontier stories and story-tellers need to claim wider spaces and that the value of honest writing in itself far outweighs the gains from its commodification. I thank them further for entrusting this book to my editor, Zinnia Sengupta. I felt like I was handing over to her a delicate loom that spun stories and needed the utmost care. Not only did she take great care but she also enhanced its weaves.

When I began writing the first story of this anthology, I realised the shortcomings in my grasp of various aspects of Assam's history. Dr Arup Jyoti Saikia's guidance and counsel were of massive help in this regard.

To Kastoori Rai Dewan, I relay my apologies for sending the first, most nascent drafts of my stories her way long before the idea of a book even took shape. Her tolerant reading and critical insights greatly motivated me to move ahead in my resolve to create this book.

Several life-altering events and episodes were interspersed with the writing of this book. One such event was my leaving India and starting humanitarian work in the Middle East. Understandably, there were moments of instability that were held together for the time being by Siddhartha Talukdar. I will always cherish the dinner I was treated to as kudos for completing the first draft of this book in Syria.

A special thanks to Paolo Comoglio, under whose leadership I understood what compassionate work spaces mean. Within such a work environment, where obliteration of the self is not demanded as an evidence of sincerity, I found the space to continue my writing.

Junjun Sharma Pathak and Danijel Cuturic remain two solid pillars, holding fort where my dual lives in the temporal world of humanitarian work and spiritual world of fiction-writing try to co-exist. Their friendship aided my writing in inexplicable ways, unknown to them both.

To my friends; Pushparaj, Shalika, Asha, Akanshya, Dikshita, Chiranjita, Rishav, Jonathan, Dima, Nawar, Hiba, Rania, Francesca, Benedicta and Sara, I remain highly indebted for their incessant encouragement of my writing and acceptance of my innate eccentricities.

Finally, for my family, my mother Noima, late father Khobir, brother Adil and aunt Nasrin, I say; nothing I would ever write here or anywhere in acknowledgement of them would suffice. Their love and support has been as perennial as the rivers that have shaped our lives, as loud as the *Bordoisila* that roars in our spring skies, and as unwavering as the esoteric gravity that pulled us together to experience this journey of life as a family. Especially my mother—she remains the centre of this gravity.